Whispers of the Silent Prophet

Holger Sontag

Whispers of the Silent Prophet

Holger Sontag

2nd Edition

Impressum

Bibliografische Information der Deutschen Nationalbibliothek: Die Deutsche Nationalbibliothek verzeichnet diese Publikation in der Deutschen Nationalbibliografie; detaillierte bibliografische Daten sind im Internet über dnb.dnb.de abrufbar.

Die automatisierte Analyse des Werkes, um daraus Informationen insbesondere über Muster, Trends und Korrelationen gemäß §44b UrhG („Text und Data Mining") zu gewinnen, ist untersagt.

© 2026 Holger Sontag

Publisher: BoD · Books on Demand GmbH, Überseering 33, 22297 Hamburg, bod@bod.de
Print: Libri Plureos GmbH, Friedensallee 273, 22763 Hamburg

ISBN: 978-3-7693-2437-2
Dieser Titel ist auch als eBook erhältlich.

Contents

I

Prologue

Galileo Galilei loved the evenings in Florence. February had already brought in the first harbingers of summer. He knew that soon the very first buds of the leaves would start to grow on the trees again. But for now, a thin layer of snow softened the sound of the horse carriages passing by his window. The air was filled with the rich aroma so typical of the end of winter. The cool moisture of the night had claimed the walls of the buildings in the streets. As he looked up, he saw not a single cloud hiding the small dots crowding the night sky. The church could say whatever it wanted. He knew that those were all distant suns and other worlds revolving around those suns, just like this one was revolving around its sun.

Last year had been exhausting for him. The church had put shackles on him, made him unable to speak the truth that he could prove. The system designed by Copernicus was worth fighting for in his mind, and his time would come. For now, he had to lay low, and that frustrated him. For tonight, he made the conscious decision to not think about it and focus on the task at hand.

The night was absolutely perfect. It was now or

never. He had envisioned a new idea. It had come to him in something of a dream. The Jupiter moons were interesting, but this was so much more than that.

He went back into his study. Piles of papers and notes had accumulated on the desk in the room. He went to the observation window where he had placed his telescope. He picked up the 1.2-meter-long tube and looked at the sky. From his dream, he knew where to turn. Standing on the little balcony, he held his telescope up to his eyes and slowly adjusted the two lenses.

Today, on the fourth of February in the year 1617, Galileo looked through his telescope and saw something new. He did not look at the moons of Jupiter as per usual these days. He looked in a different direction. A direction that up until recently had not been of any interest to him. Recently, when the dreams had started.

He looked in the direction he had learned about. No, he had dreamed about it. It was shown to him in his dreams. A cluster of stars, distant but bright. There they were. But he was astonished as he only saw three of them, not four as he remembered from his dreams. Two were brighter than the third one. He took them down in his notebook: three circles, two closer together and one further away.

1. End

Not every story has a happy ending. Many stories try to make us believe that in the end, every change leads to a resolution—hopefully a positive one. In reality, such an outcome is a rare coincidence. Most real stories do not end on a resolution of any kind. Most don't end at all. They continue long after the events of interest have played out in unforeseen ways. They may affect the protagonist in ways that diminish all that was gained when the story reaches its last page. They cause happiness after a tragic ending and pain following a happy ending. Only sometimes, in rare cases, can we grasp what will follow once we leave the story. Not because the protagonist dies or a change for an ultimately better world has occurred. We know because the hinted outcome allows us a slight peek into the world that the protagonist must now face. However, we often only understand that we could not possibly begin to understand. Yet, we do get a glimpse of the impact such a situation would have on us just before we leave the protagonist abandoned and hopeless. We put down the book and return to our peaceful lives. We remain in ignorant oblivion of the suffering, confusion, and unfathomable fear that the protagonist could experience as his story continues without prose.

-◇-

The view of the vastness of space all around him was breathtaking and humbling. McKinney knew he could never find the words to convey the depth of his feelings at that moment to anyone. The amazing image his eyes were processing only intensified his sense of dread. He tried to shake the thoughts out of his head and refocus on the task at hand. A spacewalk does not permit slander. Yet, McKinney took the liberty to allow himself a moment of respite before commencing his work. He hoped it would go unnoticed.

"Wake up, sleeping beauty! Ship to Ian, are you still out there?" The earpiece crackled a bit. Yet, McKinney clearly understood the message that Gonzales had tried to convey. Both men had known each other since the academy. They built their bond on mutual trust. It had been unbreakable since their first mission together. In fact, McKinney would likely not even be on this mission if it weren't for Gonzales. He had made a clear request for McKinney to be part of this.

"I am focused, Carlos. I just needed a minute..." That last part was more mumbled than spoken. The dreamscape that had captivated McKinney's mind for that one peaceful yet saddening moment tore him away.

The Orion Nebula had been the subject of many speculations. Some of which lacked hard evidence.

That is until about 5 years ago, when mankind first developed spaceships capable of faster-than-light travel. This made exploration of places that had been too far away for field research now possible. What McKinney saw was something no other human had ever been confronted with. He was the first person ever to come this close to the fantastic dreamscape that was the nebula. While human eyes could not make out all the vibrant colors that were assigned by deep-space photography, it was still a humbling view. All that was because of the monthly post-hop routine maintenance work on their communications array.

Many different missions had been discussed. Some had even already been planned for planets that would be closer and just as interesting. Maybe even able to sustain life. Yet, in a final decision for the first long-distance mission, the committee ultimately made its decision. The decision was to tackle the Orion Nebula first. The explanation was sparse. Funding was brought up. The photogenic appeal of the nebula had raised hopes for more impressive reports. The committee at central command wanted to sell science to fund the mission. Thus, part of their mission was providing visually stunning imagery. McKinney didn't really care for the reasoning. He understood that it would certainly spice up the new and often rather dry findings. To him, it was a grand opportunity to get a sight no human had ever had before him.

The four-man crew had started the endeavor one year ago on board the Silent Prophet. It was one of only three space vessels capable of faster-than-light travel. This, however, was the furthest expedition ever attempted, and it was not without its risks. The ships were capable of traversing great distances faster than light. But the technology was still in its infancy, and this trip was considered a trial by fire. They used a time bubble forming around the ship and tearing it out of the known universe into another space-time continuum. This concept had one detrimental flaw: the bubble did not last forever. With a buffer ensuring that the system would not overload, a distance of around 100 light years could be traversed safely. Therefore, the whole distance of around 1,350 light years was separated into fourteen hops. Each covering a specific predetermined distance. After each hop, the crew needed to check and, if necessary, repair all equipment. There was no field test for how such a prolonged exposure to the time bubble would affect the material. So after each hop, a waiting time was issued to properly ensure that the vessel was fully functional and in working order. Central command back on earth recommended a month between each hop. There was no technical reason for this.

They were on their own out here. Communication with Earth was difficult and took a long time. The last communication relay station was in the orbit of Neptune. Even with the superluminal communication the ship was capable of, it would still take years for any communication to reach Earth. The comms array made use of quantum nonlocality to cover light years within relatively short time frames. This method was incomplete. A dataframe would have to retrigger a quantum entanglement regularly to cover the full distance. It was a lifeline and a way to send regular reports, but not a way to get support for unforeseen events. The silent prophet was designed for basically maintaining itself. The crew worked through their checklists to ensure all systems did what they were designed to do. It was a protocol that was meant to be followed. However, McKinney felt his maintenance tasks were more symbolic than true necessities for the mission.

With every hop, the goal had become more visible. The crew grew increasingly excited about the prospect of performing the first real investigation of this area. The team was assigned to investigate several points of interest within the 12-light-year radius of the nebula. They would reach each point with another hop.

The Orion Nebula has been an inspiration for many myths in the past. Most notably, the Maya regarded it as the cosmic fire of creation. This was not so far from the truth. The nebula contains an unbelievably vast and ever-increasing number of new stars being born.

McKinney had the maintenance of the communications array down to a science. He knew every cable and bolt and had the exact plan of action and order of hand movements in his head. He made no unnecessary muscle contractions, and no unnecessary thoughts filled his mind. On the job, McKinney was more machine than human. Off the job, people knew him as a calm, factual, and collected person. That put him in direct opposition to Gonzales, who had always been the more lighthearted one of the two. McKinney had often thought that it was exactly because of their very different character traits that they got along so well.

"Maintenance check of the communications array complete; nothing to report." McKinney was moving back to the airlock when Gonzales's voice crackled an "affirmative" into his ears.

Before entering the ship, he once more turned towards the stunning image of the nebula that had unfolded before him. Awesome and intangible for the human mind. A colorful cloud illuminated by an unfathomable amount of flaming spheres hung in the black nothingness of space. He felt as if he could reach out his hand and touch it. His brain was not able to comprehend the distance that was still between him and the beautiful cosmic object. Then he opened the hatch door and slipped into the airlock. As the artificial gravity of the ship pulled him to the floor, the outer door closed. A hissing sound signaled a successful start to the air-cycling process.

2. Memories

It was always quite a long way down the central corridor of the ship from the airlock to the bridge. At the back of the ship was the engineering bay between the two FTL engines. The airlock was out to the right side. As he walked up the corridor, he first went past the first cross-section with the lab and med bay to the right and the crew quarters to the left. As was the case for all sectors, large pressure doors were in place to separate a section if it was damaged. The crew quarters had a large anteroom right behind the door, followed by the four small crew rooms. As McKinney walked on, he came past the second cross-section. He peeked into the mess hall that was to the left and found it to be empty. To the right was the pod room. A few meters ahead now came his destination: the bridge.

As McKinney entered, he pushed back his sweaty orange hair in a futile attempt to not look like he had been through the wringer. Reporting came first; that was protocol. A shower could be had later. As the door closed behind him with a clean swishing sound, he noticed that Gonzales was there to greet him with a wide smile. At the other end of the room, Wolf was analyzing some of the output from the ship's sensors. As usual, she was wearing the captain's uniform. Even being so far away from Earth and after so many months of travel, formality was important to her. Sometimes McKinney thought it was also because the blue uniform with gold stripes complemented her gray hair. It added some fresh color.

At the control, he saw Duong doing a final check of the ship's routing configurations. She had tied her long black hair into a knot as per usual. She was wearing the pants and shirt of her soldier uniform but had left the jacket behind. She looked up to greet McKinney. War and conflict shaped her face. Still, her beauty remained undeniable despite the small scar underneath her eye. She carried it with pride—and rightfully so.

"Welcome back, dreamer!" Gonzales was being funny. As usual, a broad smile dressed his face in delight. He had grown a well-kept beard that showed the same signs of gray hair here and there as his black hair did. McKinney knew that this would not bother Gonzales in the slightest. He was a walking sunshine.

"You have to admit, even from here, it's an astonishing view," McKinney replied as he combed through his short orange beard. "From out there, it truly is indescribable." With the other two in the room, he would normally not have been so open about his feelings. However, he was still taken aback by his experience. Already, the last few hops had been special. The closer they got to the nebula, the more extreme his feelings toward it were. He could not explain why.

"I need to report to the captain," McKinney said.

He put his hand on Gonzales's shoulder and slowly walked toward Wolf. It was a gesture that reflected brotherhood.

Seeing him approach, Wolf looked up from the ship's readouts. Her eyes were friendly and her smile warm. She had been in service for so many years, and this was likely to be her last flight. She was regarded as one of the most experienced captains the academy had ever known. Captain Astrid Wolf had more medals to her name than McKinney had years to his age. The rest of the crew regarded her almost as a mother.

"McKinney reporting back from the spacewalk. Comms are fully operational, and no repairs are needed." As he spoke, he straightened his back and made a salute with his hand. It had been a decision to uphold the least amount of militaristic discipline among the crew. It kept the people alert and prohibited slacking. Out here, in isolation, this could become a lifesaver.

Wolf returned the salute: "Thank you for the report." She said with a smile. After a moment, she added, "That must have been quite the experience this time around. I almost envy you."

McKinney tried to smile, but here it was: the situation that he had seen coming. He so wished to share his experience, but he could not possibly find words in any language ever created.

He nodded. "Impossible to describe. It was... humbling." Then he turned around and looked for Gonzales.

He found him talking to Duong, seemingly over-looking a star map. McKinney decided not to disturb the two. Gonzales did have interest in Duong despite her rough and unapproachable militaristic shell. But Gonzales was convinced that that was just for show and deep below he would find - as he put it - the heart of an angel. Additionally, Wolf had made clear that re-lationships between crewmates were strictly forbid-den. So it remained a flirt at best. This could not stop Gonzales. This journey would end at some point and then they would not be crewmates any longer. So now he was "laying a foundation," as he would call it. McKinney did not know if Duong was interested or not. She kept her stone face and focused on the mis-sion. Her long military training had made her not just a good pilot. She was disciplined to the core.

McKinney left the bridge. The door opened auto-matically and let him through before closing again af-ter him. Doors on this ship could never stay open. This was one of the many safety precautions. Should an air leak occur in any section, then the doors would with-stand the pressure easily.

Taking a rest felt like a good idea to him. He had found himself to be rather restless in the past few weeks. Sleep did not come as easily to him as it used to. Stressful situations could cause this. Gonzales had told him that in his capacity as the ship's medical doc-tor. Yes, stress had certainly weighed on him - on them all for that matter. However, currently this was only getting worse and pulling down his spirits. He did not want to burden the others, so he had not talked about it with anyone else.

-◇-

The crew quarters were the place he usually tried to avoid the most. They had been kept purposefully barren and cold. The crew needed motivation to stay together. Loneliness and isolation could become serious issues. Yet, a small amount of privacy was just necessary on an operation spanning many years. So a middle ground was found. Crew members got their own rooms, but they did not get much additional comfort.

As McKinney stepped into his room, the double sliding door closed behind him. He found himself in the shoebox that had been granted to him. On the left wall was a small closet. It was just big enough for the four sets of standard-issue clothing. On the inside was a small locker for private belongings. The opposite side of the room contained the bed with a frame welded into two ships' inner casings. The right side offered space for a small desk with a lamp and a small computer terminal on it. A chair in front of it was now circumvented by him to reach the bed, onto which he threw himself.

He did not want to sleep, but he did want to lie down. He felt exhausted. The impressions of the nebula still had not left his mind. He wanted to go out again, see it again, get closer to it. He turned to his side and tried to think of something else. However, the images kept coming back to him. With every time he felt as though he was getting closer to the nebula, he could never quite reach it. Finally, he gave up on the idea of resting and went to his desk. Focusing on something else could maybe drive away the thoughts—hopefully.

On the terminal in his room, he had stored several images and videos. The agency had allowed them to bring keepsakes and memories from their former lives on Earth. So far away from Earth, the crew should not forget their origin. Out here, it was nothing more than a thin emotional tether that was weakening with every day that passed. McKinney shuffled through old photos of things he had long lost all connection to, either by choice or by simply forgetting about them. It all seemed too distant and unrelated to him. Photos from the academy. His ex-girlfriend who had dumped him. Another ex-girlfriend whom he had dumped. That sports medal he had won in a small local running competition. The rock concert he had been at with Gonzales during their first vacation. He picked up the last item left from his father. The medal of honor that was granted to his father after he had died a hero defending space station Saturn 4 during the mutiny. McKinney had been at the academy when it happened. Back then, it had almost forced him to give up his dream. His mother's grief was deep, and he needed to care for her until her fractured heart finally gave up. The doctors said there was nothing he could have done.

All these memories painted images in his mind.

Distorted, even though he had a direct connection to all of it. But it all happened a seemingly endless time ago. The impressions of his space flights had swallowed much of the impact of many of his memories. This one in particular was almost nullifying most other experiences. In his view, it was all a gray smudge of the past.

This his heart grew heavy. What would happen if he returned home? Would all that come back? Would he let it all back in?

3. Dreams

The mess hall was purposefully the opposite of the crew quarters. Bright, somewhat cozy despite the metallic furniture. Several entertainment units were positioned alongside the walls. A place for people to meet and mingle even if the crew just consisted of four people. The room itself would easily have enough space for 15-20 enthusiastic party folks. McKinney had little interest in any of this. He was hungry, and this was the place to satisfy his need.

He noticed that he was not alone. Duong had made her way there as well, seemingly for the same purpose. McKinney walked over to the automated kitchen. A convenient machine built into the far side of the room. It would provide a ready-made meal on a plate in seconds. The reality was less stellar as there were just a few variations of the same food. The word food was used rather loosely. He punched in the code for the standard-issue protein sludge and waited for the gray-brown syrup to be splurged out onto his plastic plate. Then he decided to join Duong, who had been sitting at the central table with her back to him, visibly lost in thought.

"Mind if I join you?" he asked while sitting down.

It was a rhetorical question. With four people in the crew, what sense would it make to sit apart?

In trained muscle reflex, Duong nodded without looking up.

As McKinney put the first spoon of the gooey sustenance into his mouth, he looked at her. It was no wonder that Gonzales had an interest in her. Her beauty was undeniable. She did have a feminine fragility about her that was often hard to make out underneath the battle-hardened shell she had learned to extrude. A tough look underlined by a scar beneath her right eye. A trophy from a war McKinney had understood. There was no doubt, she was a soldier and a fighter. What she lacked in strength she would make up for in skill and experience. And yet, underneath all those years of training and fighting and killing, she could not always hide the woman that she was at heart. Lost in his train of thought, he suddenly noticed that her eyes were on him as well. Not just looking, but drilling. Little piercing daggers trying to bore into his brain. He quickly looked down at his lunch.

"So, we have made good progress..." An awkward attempt to make conversation, but the tense atmosphere in the room had gotten to him.

She kept staring him down. After a moment of silence, she asked, "You have known Gonzales for a very long time, haven't you?"

He completely ignored her question—maybe for the better. However, McKinney was becoming aware of the situation. He cursed himself for not reading the room better. Gonzales and the ladies had always been an issue in and of themselves.

"We started in the academy together," McKinney reminded himself to answer only in facts if possible.

"Has he..." she paused, "has he... always been like that?"

"Like what?" He knew what, but he still hoped for a miracle that would allow him to find an excuse to exit the conversation.

"Like... you know... hunting women?"

Yes - "no" - I lied.

McKinney was an awful liar. He hated lying. He tried to act engaged with his sludge, but he felt Duong's stare as if it had materialized into the real world and was now attacking him.

"You lied!" Her voice could not contain a certain amount of satisfaction at having seen through him. Not that it was a particularly difficult feat.

"Yes," McKinney did not look up.

"How bad was it?" she kept drilling.

"Didn't count."

"That bad, huh?" he felt her eyes again as they tried to drill further into his brain. Then she finally re-marked, "You look tired."

McKinney looked up. Now that she said it, she did look awfully tired herself. "You too." It was an inap-propriate thing to say to a lady. He was so grateful to be rid of her inquisitorial grip that he overlooked the possibility of committing another transgression.

She looked at him, and her war-weathered face

seemed to smile. Not so much by muscle activity as by radiating some form of joy that McKinney was able to somewhat receive.

"So yes, I am having a bit of a difficult time catching up on sleep. Once I do get to shut my eyes, I dream of… I dream strange things." She said with some seriousness returning to her voice.

"Same here. I talked to Gonzales; he said it is stress. I am not so sure about that… the dreams… I see a place. It's beautiful, fresh air, water, and plants everywhere. But... I don't know how to say this... It seems so... wrong somehow. It makes me feel uneasy."

"It seems distorted." She added.

McKinney looked at her. He felt spooked. How can two people from such completely different backgrounds have such identical dreams? "Y… Yes, I cannot say why. It doesn't feel real in the dream. I know how that sounds, but I don't know how else to describe it."

Duong nodded absent minded. Finally she added, "I thought so."

"What does it mean?" asked McKinney.

"I don't know, but we are on an adventure that no human has ever been on. Maybe our imagination is just running wild?" she said to calm herself. It was no explanation for why both of them had similar dreams, but she had no explanation either way. As she spoke, she got up and picked up her plate, clearly signaling that she was about to leave.

McKinney nodded in return and went back to

stuffing another spoonful of slime into his mouth.

-◇-

Engineering did not allow for much manual labor. The faster-than-light (or FTL, for short) engine core was out of physical reach. A human could never withstand the radiation for any amount of time. The maintenance needed to be done completely by the use of robotic arms. The life support systems were distributed throughout the whole ship. They could only be analyzed using the digital readouts. In essence, there was not much that needed any kind of immediate checkup that the self-analysis could not track down. The construction of the ship was kept purposefully simple. This limited McKinney's work to pretty much that of IT maintenance. The only part that actually needed a manual checkup was the comms relay on the outside of the ship.

His last task before a hop was always a final checkup, especially of the FTL core. The hop would begin in a little less than an hour, but McKinney was anyway almost finished.

As he overlooked the final readouts on the screen for any anomalies, Duong entered the room.

"Sorry to disturb you, but..."

Without turning around, he completed her sentence: "… there is no plausible explanation for us two sharing the same strange dream."

"Yes, there simply isn't." Her voice sounded

exhausted and out of character. Was she that shaken? Or just tired?

On that note, McKinney felt the need to turn around and look her in the face. The moment she noticed his motion, she immediately tried to pull the militaristic mask back over her face as she had trained for many years. Her face straightened out. Her eyes became sharp as ever. Yet, a slight crack in her demeanor would not vanish completely. McKinney was not the best at reading people, but he understood that she was genuinely concerned.

"Yes, it is certainly quite the mystery," he said slowly, attempting to remove all concern from his voice.

He turned around again, hoping to give her some space. Perhaps he was hoping she would come up with an explanation.

Finally, McKinney broke the silence: "Look, maybe it has to do with… seeing that…" he pointed at one of the walls. The room did not have windows to actually show what he was talking about, yet it was obvious what he meant. "That nebula out there is imprinting on my mind. I have been thinking about it. About what new worlds we will discover. What new scientific insights humanity will be able to gain. It is keeping my mind occupied. That has to have some effect."

Duong tilted her head slightly to the side. McKinney knew that what he had said was probably nonsense. However, the next hop was about to start, and he had to finish his work and put his mind at ease—at least somewhat.

"Come, we need to get ready." McKinney's words were an attempt to end an awkward moment, and it worked. Duong was back to her dutiful, militaristic self the moment the situation demanded it of her. She was a professional. Gonzales would have a tremendously difficult time cracking that shell. McKinney laughed internally, thinking about it.

Duong nodded and stepped out of the room and marched off. As the door closed behind her, McKinney took a few moments to gather his thoughts. The dreams had gotten more intense with each hop. They always started similarly: a distant vision of the nebula. In it, the four-star constellation known as the Trapezium was shining with brilliance and clarity. Then a pull of unimaginable speed hurdled him through empty space towards the Trapezium. An abrupt stop. Then he stands in a lush meadow, breathing in fresh air. As he lifts his head, a tremendous landscape is revealed. Beautiful and perfect. But there is something wrong. It feels... uncanny, unreal. It does not feel like something his mind could create. There is a distortion.

McKinney took himself out of his thoughts. With a head shake, he reminded himself to return to work. There was not much left to do anyway, but he needed to be meticulous and go through all the details carefully. A mistake could be detrimental. He refocused himself and went back to work.

McKinney had finished and sent his report to Wolf. She would now enter her activation code on the bridge to start the sequence. With her approval, they could execute the hop as planned. An instant traversal of a hundred light years. An awesome feat of human engineering. As he entered the pod room, Wolf, Duong, and Gonzales were already activating their hop pods. Neither spoke a word. McKinney directly went to his hop pod and got ready. The pods were human-sized capsules aligned on the right side of the room. They had a metal casing with a glass canopy. Inside a foam embedding that was perfectly shaped for a specific person. Interchanging them was impossible. The first one at the back of the room was optimized for Wolf. Next to her would be Gonzales. Then McKinney. At the entrance, closest to the door, was Duong's pod. It was closest to the emergency ship controls in the room. On the right side was a gigantic screen attached to a minimal set of controls. These could, if needed, perform emergency maneuvers on the ship. The giant screen now showed - as always - the countdown till the start of the next hop.

During a hop, the human body would be torn apart atom by atom by the forces of space and time that collide around the bubble. Hop pods essentially created a small personal bubble within the ship's bubble. It was much stronger and managed to contain the body within its own space-time continuum. This one was relative to the bubble the ship maintained but much more stable. The stability was possible as it did not have to move like the main bubble. It only had to maintain its relative position on a much smaller scale. By no means did that transform a hop into a comfortable situation to be in. The sudden tearing created by time slowing down was still very actively felt. Despite the effect being toned down to a level where a human can survive it. However, it was a painful procedure and very taxing for the body and mind. That is why the pod also sedated the user and relaxed his muscles. When waking up, all that remains was a feeling of disorientation and a muscle ache. McKinney had already gotten used to it after the fourth hop.

McKinney stepped into his pod last. He did not look forward to this. He always had the fear of the sedative not working or his body getting too used to it, hence lowering its effect. As the pod closed, he looked over to Gonzales, who was already breathing in the sleeping gas. On his other side was Duong, who was already asleep. She had methods that soldiers apparently learn for falling asleep faster. She explained it once to them; McKinney's mind did not accept the concept and thus he had forgotten. The routing computer now initiated his sleeping time and then started the countdown to the scheduled hop. McKinney's last thought, before he fell asleep, was of the big timer on the opposite wall. As his sedative did its work, the numbers began to fade. Finally, sleep released him to the now-familiar free fall through space. The

Trapezium lit up before he was again torn off his feet and pulled away towards it at unimaginable speed. This time, below him appeared not long after the strange landscape. He decided to look around. He never did try that. Usually, the dream would end here. This time it would not. He tried to lift his feet. The ground gave way. Something was suddenly moving beneath him. As he looked down, he saw something at his feet. A distortion shattered the ground beneath him. As if the dream ended here and something intangible began. He tripped and fell into empty space.

4. Alteration

The hop went as planned. As the sedative wore off, McKinney slowly opened his eyes. It looked as though he was the first one awake this time. He sometimes wondered what was determining the exact time of awakening. The dosage seemed to be high enough to easily outlast any hop. Then he noticed movement in Gonzales Pod. Tired, his hands went for the button that would unseal the pod and release him. His practiced hand felt its way around the soft inner buffer material. His fingers only felt the uneven surface of the cushioning where he had expected the button to be. It had to be there—but it simply wasn't. A panic overcame him. A rush of adrenaline flushed out the remaining numbness. He struggled with his hands and tried to look down through the narrow opening between him and the pod wall. No button... desperately, he looked for help to the left and right of him. He only found the same confusion in the faces of his colleagues. Then he shifted his head to the other side. There it was as if it had always been there. The button—had it moved? But how could that even be possible? Had his memory played a trick on him? No, that meant it had played a trick on them all.

What was happening? McKinney thought to himself as he pushed the button and watched the seal open. It released the internally chambered and pressurized gases as a hissing cloud of steam. He climbed out and looked around. Duong had also already left the pod, and Wolf's pod was just opening. Gonzales was still in the pod and looked at McKinney with a frustrated face. Then he, too, pushed the button. McKinney could already make out his words before hearing them. However, he was more focused on finding out if he was more concerned about the placement of the button, or about the fact that the placement of the button didn't concern him a lot more. McKinney felt as if he should be severely worried. However, something put his mind at ease—at least to a degree.

"What is going on here?" Gonzales's voice echoed in everyone's heads.

-◇-

Maintenance was a lot more important after the experience with the pods. The whole crew had agreed on performing an instant checkup of all systems. The existence of other abnormalities needed to be verified—or hopefully dismissed. The part that made this occurrence bewildering was the complete lack of evidence for manipulation. The only hint was a slight distortion around the button and its connection. Under close inspection, McKinney realized the surface was ever so slightly malformed. It seemed to have been changed on a molecular level by someone who had a disorderly idea of how to arrange molecules. The button itself looked like it had always been there. No sign of tinkering here. On the surface, the new arrangement looked as if it had been designed from the ground up to be in that place. All cabling and connectors were perfectly aligned inside the pods. McKinney could not wrap his head around this, and he was afraid of what could be next. If everything had changed on the ship, how long would it take them to figure out how to regain control?

His mind was wandering in all kinds of different directions as he walked toward the airlock at the rear of the ship. It was an unpredictable horror scenario. Maybe they were already stranded outside of communication range to Earth. He sealed his helmet and slowly walked toward the airlock.

The moment the outside hatch opened, McKinney immediately saw it. So much closer, so much more humbling. The Silent Prophet now hung in space so unbelievably close to the Orion Nebula that it filled McKinney's complete vision. Even if he turned around, he could still make out its shine. The colors were now much more vibrant and otherworldly. He noticed how the nebula was inconsistent, warped, and distorted ever so slightly as he looked at it. It was an awesome and deeply impressive view.

As if torn from slumber, the crackling of his headset made him aware of the fact that he had stood there for almost 15 minutes. For those 15 minutes, he had been staring deeper and deeper into the nebula. Gonzales's voice was a reminder of a reality he had almost forgotten: "Get a move on!"

"Yes, sorry," he mumbled into the helmet microphone and scrambled up the side of the ship toward the communications array.

-◇-

A quick surface-level inspection revealed nothing out of the ordinary. McKinney felt a sense of relief. As long as communications were up, they could work through most problems. If there were changes under the hood, they had at the very least done no irreparable damage. He opened the main maintenance panel on the side to expose the switchboards and cabling. Going through the different contact points all seemed to be as expected—except that something felt off. He decided to go through everything again as he could not shake the feeling of having missed something important.

Then it hit him: the labels.

He squinted his eyes. He had gone through maintenance of the comms array so often by now that he did not even look at them anymore. He did not even remember when he had last consciously read them. However, he knew that the labels had to be wrong, or was his mind wrong? The text on them was most definitely not English as it used to be. Maybe not even a language he had ever seen before. Chaotic scribbles replaced some of the letters, making them resemble no human language.

He could not help but stare at the obscure symbols or runes that had taken the place of the short words. Where it used to say conductors, processors, or transistors, he saw only strange images. From memory, he could reconstruct what each of the labels meant. He found no evidence of tinkering with the technical components themselves.

Unsure what to report, he closed the unit up again and made his way to the airlock - the nebula looming over him. Averting his gaze from the hatch. He froze again to feast his eyes on the endless play of chaotic lights. His eyes wanted to capture the phenomenon in its complete beauty. Grasp every ray of light, latch on to every celestial body, and name every single one of the otherworldly colors. He did not notice that his mind started to float through space, drawn in by... something in the nebula.

Then something suddenly pulled on his belt sharply and tore his mind away from the alluring depth of the nebula and back into reality. A cold shiver went down his spine. Unknowingly, he had let go of the handles on the ship's exterior and was now only attached via a safety cord. As quickly as he could, he reeled himself back on deck. His mind almost frozen from fear, he pushed himself through the hatch as fast as possible. After the outside hatch shut behind him, the air-cycling system of the airlock came to life. With the well-known hissing sound of the decontamination gas,

McKinney managed to get his heart rate down again little by little. Then the gas was sucked out again and the radiation levels normalized. Finally, as air was pushed back into the chamber, he found some mental stability again. He took off the heavy spacesuit and placed it back into the glass casket next to the airlock door. While still closing the zipper of his jacket, he went toward the bridge to report his findings. He was a factual man. He would report in detail what he saw, no matter how strange it seemed to him.

-◇-

"I don't even see a pattern," Wolf said as McKinney entered. She was standing around the tactical desk with Gonzales and Duong. On the desk was a sizable pile of printouts—clearly unsorted. McKinney cared little about the paper. He was too much in disbelief at Wolf's voice. It had shifted, ever so slightly, from her usually controlled tone. This might have been the very first time he ever saw a hint of Wolf losing her composure. She was upset, and she seemed nervous. Nervous to such an extent that she could not manage to keep it to herself under the high amount of control McKinney was used to seeing.

As McKinney approached the table, Gonzales greeted him: "You have come at just the right time. Take a look at this."

He handed McKinney a seemingly random sheet of paper from the table. McKinney looked at it, and at first, it looked like a normal readout. But as he looked closer, he saw them. Without rhyme or reason, here and there they were strewn about. It was the exact same symbols McKinney had seen on the labels of the comms array. Here, they were replacing parts of the text. He quickly understood the problem. The symbols were not added, but instead, they replaced words, maybe even complete sections. The whole log was essentially unusable at this point. A crushing feeling surged through his body. Without a word, he handed the paper back to Gonzales and ran toward the engineering bay. He had to see if this affected the entire machinery. If it did, then he had no way of knowing if the FTL engine was damaged or not. They would be in grave danger.

As he stepped through the door, the automated light came alive and illuminated the room with its cold, pale, colorless brightness. He went to the main console and started punching in the necessary access codes for the different maintenance sensors and systems. The current readouts on the screen looked completely okay. A sigh of relief left his lips. Without the logs, it was all just hoping and praying. On such a high-risk mission, solely relying on a benevolent higher power never proved to be a good idea. It seemed to affect only printed text. Text in digital form seemed to be free of this issue.

He went back to the bridge. Wolf had apparently started to categorize the readouts.

"Check the screen," said McKinney as he stepped

closer. "It only affects printed materials."

Wolf looked up. There was something in her eyes that made McKinney question his resolve to step closer. Wolf got up and went for the screens. She slowly pressed the necessary buttons, and after a few moments, text appeared. Normal text. Flawless text.

She turned around and gave McKinney a stern look. After a while, she finally spoke: "Okay, we have the readouts, but that does not explain what is going on here." Her voice was back under her complete control. She returned to the table and grabbed a small pile of paper to hold it up and shake it with her right hand. "This should not happen. It must mean something. This is a science vessel. Researching the nebula is our job. As far as I am concerned, all this has something to do with the nebula. Let us put our efforts into understanding what is going on. That also means maintenance checks must continue as planned, so ensure we are ready for whatever may happen. We will have to see if this affects our mission in any way or if we can proceed as planned. I will inform home base."

Since the very start of the mission, Wolf had not been this nervous. Her voice had an unnatural and forced calmness to it. So much so that McKinney felt a shiver moving up his spine from just listening. He decided it was better to leave the table. Something within him stopped him from making a report right then and there. He only knew that he needed to calm himself down. Subjecting himself to the stress that was slowly bubbling up in and around the table would not be helpful.

As McKinney was at the door that swiftly opened for him, he looked back. Wolf was gathering all the documents off the table and putting them under her arm.

The ship would not check itself. He decided to go back to the engineering bay. This time for an actual analysis of whatever it was that was going on. Maybe the ship's systems would give at least a hint of what was happening. He stepped out and, behind him, the door closed with a soft swishing sound.

5. Leap

After the past days, stepping back into the hop pod came with great unease for McKinney. A million questions crashed into his mind. The order to proceed came highly unexpectedly. Everyone was certain Wolf would call off the mission under these circumstances. But instead, she announced that they would proceed as planned.

"This has always been a mission into the unknown. We are explorers. Humanity expects us to explore new horizons even if it gets dangerous or difficult. I expect that we will handle this professionally. Each one of you should ensure that we are ready for further distortions of text. Make us independent of printed labels, texts, and whatever else you can find. This mission will proceed as planned."

Her voice had been stern, focused, and clear. Nobody in the crew doubted her. Yet, he still wondered why Wolf had taken all the printouts into her room and locked the door. She had spent significant amounts of time in that room, away from the rest of the crew. She had been preparing her logbooks and protocols, she had said. However, she had seemed very distracted whenever he spoke to her. He did not feel good about the situation, but he trusted her fully to make the best decisions. So, he followed her orders—for now.

His part of the preparations has gone over fairly quickly. Using a datapad, he has spent only a few hours digitizing all manuals and labels. For the last few days, he had helped Gonzales. The labels of the medication bottles and boxes had been affected to the degree that single letters were changed or exchanged. Gonzales had immediately taken action and digitized all medication labels. Additionally, he had noted down the exact location of each bottle—in digital writing and on film. For bottles that looked too similar, he had added extra markings on the glass itself. He had borrowed McKinney's laser cutter for that. He had then relocated them far away from each other. He wanted to have as much certainty as possible that he would not make any mistakes. Nobody knew what could change with another hop, so Gonzales wanted to be as prepared as possible.

McKinney had helped Duong as well.

"I am not sure if something really had changed on the flight controls. They look like I remember them. Even the labels seem intact - and yet... Something is not right," she had told him. McKinney had also thought that something was just ever so slightly off. He had looked over the consoles for similar distortions as he had seen on the pod, and he had found minor traces. Yet it was impossible to say what exactly had been affected as the buttons all seemed to do what Duong remembered they should do. They worked just fine, and nothing was missing or clearly out of place, so they decided to greenlight it.

All this and more should have made McKinney not want to get any closer to the nebula. Yet, he did not resist the decision for the next hop. Something in him was genuinely excited about it.

-◇-

As the sedative did its duty and slumber successfully reached out to McKinney. It was now dragging him ever deeper into an unknown and surreal world. He felt like something was different this time around.

Again, he was pulled onto the strange but beautiful planet. Again, he was alone. But then he was back in the pod room on board the Silent Prophet—and yet he was still on that planet. It was not an overlap. Dream and reality were bleeding into each other. The place was both places at once and yet neither of them. It was a place that could not exist in reality. Yet, it felt tangible as if in this dimension the concept of reality was different and logically allowed such a construct. He felt ill to his stomach as his brain tried to comprehend what he was seeing. It was as if the human mind was not designed for witnessing a vista such as this.

As he stood in the room and in the meadow, he noticed that things around him were ever-changing. It was not a fixed place. It was a chaotic combination that was constantly in disarray. It was reshaping and reconfiguring itself into different chaotic and random amalgamations. Here, a few branches of a tree were mimicking the emergency control console. There, a batch of tall grass was actually one of the hop pods. The crystal-clear lake was actually the massive wall clock ticking up, not down. As he stepped closer forward the distortion reshaped reality around him further and suddenly his own pod grew out of nothingness into existence - even recreating... him. As he looked, he could also make out the silhouettes of Gonzales and Duong. Somehow, his eyes were trying to create shapes that his mind could comprehend and the distortions became worse. He felt a pain arising. He felt his eyes and mind were strained beyond their capability. His body was not capable of processing this environment and he suffered for it.

He rubbed his eyes as they teared up. It became increasingly difficult for him to see and make out details around him. It all felt so real—or unreal to him. He tried to cling to objects he knew and stumbled even closer to his pod. As he touched it, he could not help but notice that it felt like metal and glass. It was there, cold to the touch. Suddenly he heard a noise, a static droning or humming. An electric conductor or a coil whine? He slowly felt his way towards the sound. As he stepped forward, he noticed that darkness was starting to envelop his vision. It swallowed all light until he was standing in absolute darkness. As he tried to find his footing, his hands touched the cold, metallic surface of a part of the ship. Grasping the object, McKinney noticed that his hands were moving across the surface of a hop pod. Upon closer inspection, he realized that it was the hop pod of Wolf. All throughout, the pressure of the hum had been growing in his head. The sound was now everywhere around him, an endless distortion noise pressing on his mind and pushing into his thoughts.

Suddenly, in the corner of his eye, he noticed movement. He was not alone; something was inside the darkness. He quickly jerked his head around and saw... nothing. Darkness. He stepped closer to see more. Around him, all light had abandoned the place. He could barely see more than 1 meter far. Carefully he put one foot in front of the next. Something swiped across his face. It felt like an electric cable had touched his skin. Where he felt it, the air swirled in chaotic ways, as if the molecules had lost their binding. In panic, he touched his face where the cable had slid over his skin. He felt slight ripples, as if his skin molecules had become rearranged. As he continued to feel them, the ripples evened out. It felt like a temporary distortion of his skin molecules.

His curiosity pushed him forward. It was clear to him that whatever had caused that had also caused the distortion of the texts and the shift of the button. He was cautious. The disruption had been temporary, but he reminded himself that the button and the text had been changed permanently. Slowly, his hands grabbed into the air in front of him as he placed one foot in front of the other. He did not know if he was going in the right direction, or if whatever had been there was still there. Yet he felt a presence somewhere close to him. Suddenly, he could make out something directly at his fingertips. He could not see it, but his fingers were moving across something. It felt electric and cold. The surface was rippled as if wrapped in hundreds of thin tubes that were constantly moving. He could not grab them or hold onto them. It all felt volatile. He went closer.

Then his hands again reached into nothing. The darkness retreated. The reality around him shifted. He was again on the luscious green planet. The small waterfall softly bedded crystal-clear droplets in a calm little lake. A warm wind caressed the tall grass that slowly danced in perfect synchronicity. Trees that would harbor playful critters and colorful birds. They sang the most beautiful songs. A perfect world that could never exist.

He knew he was not alone. He knew he was being watched. He felt their gaze. A piercing cold gaze.

The wailing of the siren tore McKinney out of the fake reality of his dream. He had not known how loud a siren could be up until now. The hop had stopped as the safety measures kicked the ship out of the bubble. There was no subtlety to this maneuver. McKinney was internally impressed and grateful for it.

Torn from his nightmare, he had difficulty finding himself. The pod auto-ejected him as is protocol during such emergencies. The complete crew must be woken up. It was important to ensure that any emergency could be taken care of. The big screen that usually displayed the clock now showed a fatal error message:

POD 1 COMPROMISED!

He was still numb and confused from what he had just experienced. As he scrambled to his feet, he noticed that Gonzales was already moving towards Wolf's pod. McKinney envied Gonzales's capability for fast recovery. They had trained for this for months before the start, but McKinney had never achieved the times of Gonzales. That man had infinite energy, not just when pursuing women.

Struggling to stay on his feet, McKinney maneuvered his body consciously in the direction of Wolf's pod. There was no grace in his movement, but grace was not important. So he stumbled across the room to where Gonzales was already helping Wolf out of her pod. She did not speak. She looked confused and bewildered around. Seemingly struggling to recognize her crew. Her forehead was bleeding.

"What happened?" McKinney asked.

"Not sure. It seems she tried to exit her pod." Gonzales did not just appear awake. His body and mind were working at full capacity, and McKinney was glad for it.

McKinney looked at Wolf. The wound on her

forehead was still dripping. A fine stream of blood now ran down her forehead into her gray hair, turning it crimson while vanishing between the hair strands. She looked with scared eyes at Gonzales. Then suddenly she tried to struggle free of Gonzales's tight grip, but her efforts were weak. Soon her body went limp and gave up. Gonzales managed to fully pull her out of the pod with McKinney's help. They placed Wolf on the floor, leaning against the pod. Gonzales was kneeling next to her, checking her vitals as best he could to get a first impression.

Duong was standing a little aside and watching the whole situation unfold silently. Her face was impossible to read. She was in total control of herself at that moment. Her training had taken over her demeanor. She fully understood her responsibilities and analyzed the situation. She had to find out what potential danger had caused this. After all, she was responsible for the safety of the crew. McKinney noticed how her eyes shifted to the pod from time to time. He decided to take a closer look once Wolf was in stable condition.

"Could you get a stretcher from medical?" Gonzales had looked at Duong. She hesitated for just a moment before turning around and marching off toward the door. Med bay was just down the corridor. It would not take long for her to return.

As Duong arrived with the stretcher Wolf started to move a little and mumbled: "No need... I only need a... a second." She then proceeded to struggle back to her feet. Gonzales helped her as best he could. McKinney made way and looked at her with deep concern.

"Let us go to the med bay. I want to at least take care of the wound." Gonzales was persistent, and Wolf gave in, still staggering on unstable legs. They left the room slowly, and McKinney wondered if he should help but decided that Gonzales was the right person to handle the situation. So he stayed behind to get his head out of the lingering slumber first.

McKinney looked at Duong. She had slowly moved closer to the pod. McKinney followed her. It became pretty obvious from where the head wound originated. The pod's hardened glass window had a golf-ball-sized blood splash. A few streams ran from it towards the bottom of the canopy. McKinney wondered how it was possible to even reach the glass with the head. The body was strapped in by the soft buffer material from shoulder to shoulder. The head was usually fixed to both sides. In the worst case, it would nod forward a little until again caught by a buffer cushion. He looked over to Duong. Her eyes were fixed on the cushion inside the pod that was designed to keep the head in place on the left side. Then McKinney saw it too. Part of the cushion material looked different from the rest. It had the same signature of distortion that they had seen on the other changed materials. A ripple where the structure was changed on a molecular level. He then found a similar structure on the outside of the pod around the same area. Had something tried to enter? Did this cause the alert? He remembered his dream. Something was near Wolf's pod. It struck him and changed reality around him. And now the reality of Wolf's pod had changed. The coincidence was staggering, but how could that be true? He wanted to quickly discard the idea, but it lingered.

"Such nonsense," he mumbled to himself, hoping that saying it out loud would help his mind accept a different reality. Duong looked at him knowingly. Words were clearly not needed, but he still felt the urge to at least bring up the topic. He slowly moved his head to face Duong and simply asked, "Dream?"

She nodded.

McKinney had the rising feeling that he was slowly but surely losing his mind.

6. Stormfront

Wolf was already back up and had rebuilt her facade to near perfection. A small band-aid on the left side of her forehead was seemingly the only grim reminder of the occurrences that had happened only a few hours ago. They had lunch together in the mess. Usually a lively occasion. Lately, things had become quieter. Today especially, nobody wanted to say anything. Everyone stared down at their formless nutrition-sludge. McKinney had the feeling that it had gotten a lot more disgusting to look at than ever before.

Earlier, they had wanted to visit Wolf on med. However, she had already left and vanished into her room. So McKinney had tried to get information from Gonzales on what happened. He had looked his old friend directly in the eyes and simply said, "I think you already know what happened." McKinney recalled the dream. Did Gonzales have the same dream? Could that have been it?

This was still lingering in his mind. What did he see in that dream? Was it real? How did reality and dream intermingle like that? He peered over to Gonzales and poked his fork into the slimy substance in front of him. Steered by muscle memory, he shoveled up a small pile of goop and brought it to his mouth. He then somehow managed to persuade his body to accept the sludge and welcome it into his stomach. Yet today his stomach felt small. Way too small to hold even this small heap of moist, wobbly matter. So he set his fork down again and lifted his head instead, staring right at Wolf. She had not spoken ever since she entered the mess hall.

"Captain, we saw a... Well... An anomaly... near your head cushion. Do you have any recollection of what happened?" Gonzales wanted to speak, yet Wolf motioned him to sit down.

"No. All I remember is pieces of a dream - no explanation for what happened." Wolf spoke the words slowly and moved her attention back to her slimy pile of edible mud.

Now the topic was hanging in the room, and McKinney needed to know so much more. He decided to drill into Gonzales once more after they had eaten. Maybe exchanging what had happened in the dream could help.

Wolf continued watching McKinney from across the table. She took her time with the mouthful she was currently trying to work down her throat. Eventually, the bizarre display of played enjoyment of the edible substance found its crescendo. Finally, Wolf moved her attention fully back to McKinney: "I only had a dream, nothing more. Maybe there is a perfectly technical reason for the malformed cushion. Please do get to work on fixing it before the next hop. No need for a second bump on the head." She pointed at her little bandage and got up from her chair.

"I dreamed of something being at your drop pod. It attacked me as well." He had tried to avoid that topic. However, now that Wolf had repeatedly mentioned her dream, he felt that clarifying it would be necessary.

He noticed that after he had spoken, there was complete silence in the room. Gonzales looked like he wanted to say something but decided not to. Duong kept her eyes focused on the oddity covering her plate.

Wolf collected her plate from the table and went towards the tray return at the food processor. While depositing her leftovers in the garbage, she began to speak: "We are going through a lot of stress with our minds acting up. None of us has been sleeping well. Speaking of which, you should all get some rest for now. The system maintenance can wait until tomorrow."

As she passed by McKinney, he noticed a small ripple at the back of her head, ever so slightly visible between her hair strands.

-◇-

It was late and the past few days had been relentless. McKinney had spent almost three days non-stop repairing Wolf's pod. Despite the direct order, he found it more important to ensure that the pod was in perfect order in case they needed to escape from here quickly.

He had suppressed his urge to go outside and see the nebula, but it had always lingered. This gave him the energy to work for almost three days and nights without a break. As he finished, he was overcome by exhaustion. Gonzales had told him that he would not allow him outside without rest first. McKinney had felt angry about the situation. He wanted to finally go out and see the nebula. However, he then realized that his level of exhaustion was much greater than he had realized. So he had dragged himself to his room. Now McKinney wanted to make the best use of his first break in these three days to quickly get this over with. His bed felt foreign as he dropped himself onto the unused sheets.

After staring into empty space for a while, he realized that he would not be able to remain calm enough to fall asleep. In reality, he did not want to sleep. He was lying on his bed and the only thing on his mind was the nebula. In such a quiet downtime, its relentless beauty had fully cleared his mind of all other thoughts. He wanted to go out again, to get closer, to see, to feel. One more hop and he would finally be inside the nebula. It would surround him like the embrace of a loving mother. A mother who was there for him when he needed her. A mother who was not broken and needed him to lay down his dreams for her. These thoughts made him feel warm and comfortable. A feeling he had longed to harbor for a long time. He curled up on his bed. Finally easing his mind into much-needed rest.

A knock on the door disrupted his dreams and tore him out of the motherly embrace. He felt rage swelling up inside him. This was unlike him. He tried to calm his mind before answering.

"What?" His tone was still filled with more anger than he had hoped for. Whoever was on the outside was wondering that as well, as it took a few moments until a muffled answer was audible from behind the door.

It was Duong's voice. Rough and militaristic: "We need to talk, McKinney."

McKinney sighed and got up from his bed into a seated position. He felt a lot colder than he should feel. He rubbed his hands together to create some warmth, noticing that he wasn't actually cold. The rooms all had a comfortable temperature all the time, so it was all just in his mind.

"Please come in." He was back in full control of his feelings. His tone was now a lot calmer and more collected; the anger had not fully vanished, but he managed to swallow it whole.

The door slid open with the familiar swishing sound, and Duong entered the room. Behind her, the door closed again, and she took her seat in McKinney's chair without asking him. Then, for a while, she just sat there staring at him, as if she were waiting for something to happen. Then a second knock was heard at the door.

Without waiting for McKinney to broadcast another invitation, Gonzales opened the door and stepped in. The door slid back into its closed position as Gonzales pushed Duong to the side softly. He sat down on the cupboard that was welded against the wall of the tiny room. As she looked back, their eyes met. Neither seemed to want to let go of that moment even at a time like this. McKinney felt alien in his own room. He had been so busy that he didn't notice directly that Gonzales and Duong had been sticking together closely since the last hop. Was this really the right time for starting a romance? He guessed that the heart wouldn't really care for the circumstances that set it ablaze. Still, both were professionals in their field and clearly understood the assignment. Whatever had sparked between them would have to wait until their return.

After the very short but tremendously revealing moment had passed, Gonzales turned to McKinney, who was trying to appear invisible or at least distracted. He wanted no part in this. Gonzales had always caused trouble for himself and McKinney for just a few moments of satisfaction in the academies' dorms. It had generally been illegal, and Gonzales had generally not cared.

On one especially bad occasion, McKinney had gotten pushed out of the room by Gonzales and his orbital mathematics professor, Mrs. Amarok. She was a looker despite her age, and Gonzales had been on the hunt. Now McKinney was a co-conspirator. He had seen it all. He knew about the details, and he was unable to talk. This all came down on him once Mr.

Amarok had found out about the affair and looked for evidence to use in the divorce case. McKinney had been physically threatened by the large, burly man and his even larger friend. They wanted him to speak out in court, and the academy's principal had invited him to an interview on the matter as well. This whole issue had gotten Gonzales a one-year-long suspension and McKinney six months. However, these punishments had been revoked less than a week later at the request of one of the bigger shareholders of the academy: a rich British widow by the name of Mrs. Bennett. Gonzales had known her as well - probably extremely well. That much McKinney was sure of.

Clearly, Gonzales had gotten older but none the wiser. Here he was again about to break protocol and again McKinney was a co-conspirator. Maybe Mrs. Bennett would help him out here as well when Wolf found out and had them euthanized.

"I checked the hop logs," Duong finally brought forth. The words came out strong and clear. And pulled McKinney out of the past back into the present.

"I checked the documentation I had created for all medication, Ian," Gonzales continued the discussion.

McKinney was now curious: "... and?"

"The logs are completely unreadable," Duong stated.

"You mean the prints?" McKinney asked, although he feared that he already knew what was going on.

"No, the digital logs," Duong confirmed McKinney's fear. This was somehow expected but truly terrifying. McKinney did not even know how to respond. After spending days repairing Wolf's hop pod, he did not have time yet to check the communications array as he should have. Now he was all the more concerned and became a lot more nervous about his spacewalk.

"The medication labels are also fully unreadable. So is my digital documentation, Ian," Gonzales added. This was something McKinney would have been able to guess at this point.

"The reordering, did that help?" McKinney asked Gonzales.

"It did to a degree. However, for some vials I am not completely sure... We should be fine on that end... Hopefully." Gonzales made his voice sound strong. As 2nd in command and Wolf somewhat out of commission, he needed to be a leader now. He had stepped forward to that degree and fulfilled his duties. He coordinated the small team well. Yet McKinney knew that he could not expect a solution from Gonzales on this matter. Wolf was a decision maker, and as long as she was around, she would make these decisions. A steady fix point McKinney could rely on. But that reminded him that he had not seen Wolf for all those three days.

"Where is Wolf?" McKinney asked.

"I assume she's in her room. We tried knocking but got no answer," Duong said.

So Gonzales was now in charge? This shocked McKinney more than he would have admitted. He needed to free up his mind, and the only thing he could think of that would allow him to do so was again staring into the endless beauty of the nebula.

"I will go out now and check the comms. Maybe we can figure something out. No sense in sitting here pondering; we will not find a solution in this room." McKinney had jumped up from his bed. The thought of getting out to the nebula had given him back a lot of energy.

Gonzales and Duong remained put. McKinney could not get past them without them getting up first. They were blocking him from witnessing the true beauty of the universe. How dare they? Again, he felt anger growing within him.

Regaining control over his facial muscles, he asked, "Can you let me pass?"

Duong stared a while longer at him, then she said, "You behave like an addict, McKinney." But then she gave way hesitantly.

McKinney did not even care about what she had said. Important was that he could now see the nebula. He immediately squeezed past Gonzales and the chair and left the room. He felt their stares as the door closed behind him. No time to waste. He had to slow himself down to not run. Despite all the things that were happening on board, he suddenly felt happy and free.

7. Storm

With every hop closer to the nebula, something in McKinney started screaming louder to just stop and stare. To let go, to float away. Something inside of him conjured the wish to enter the nebula. He wished to be surrounded by it, to be fully consumed by the unspeakable beauty. There was also a second voice. One that was much quieter. One he rarely ever truly heard. At this very moment, however, that small voice became loud enough to be audible. It screamed. It screamed in terror and agony. It screamed at McKinney to run away. Then it was again silenced as he left the airlock and stepped outside into a world of unimaginable wonder. A world where divine magic erased all competing thoughts from McKinney's mind. He did not even bother to move forward. Fully sucked in by the astonishing and unparalleled spectacle that was now so close. Less than a few light-years away. He could now fully make out thousands upon thousands of stars that had been born in this otherworldly flame of life. His eyes shifted around in awe. Trying to take it all in. To follow every star, to understand every construct.

Then suddenly, the stars shifted. A bright beam of

light cut through the peaceful silence. It consumed everything in its path. In pain, McKinney held his gloved hands in front of his helmet to shield his eyes as best he could. The light was so bright that it shone right through his gloves, and he could make out the skeletal structure of his hands. He threw his body to the side and buried his face between the ship's steel plating and whatever body parts he could add. His only thought was to face away from the light. Then finally, it was over again. After a while, he got back up. His eyes were not yet able to make out much. He decided to wait for a bit longer. His surroundings were still blurry. He could only make out light and dark and basic shapes.

Then he looked up and saw it.

The Trapezium. The heart of the nebula.

So bright, so clearly visible despite his faulty vision.

It was the source of all light. The source of all life. The source of all!

He noticed the image clearing up further as his eyes slowly regenerated. The brightness started to hurt again. McKinney averted his gaze again and scrambled to his feet. He needed to move. Everything was still too bright, but he felt as though he could not stay outside much longer.

Approaching the comms array, he already noticed the changes. In fact, he hardly even recognized what he was looking at. One thing was for certain: it was no longer designed for communication. Still, he was curious and stepped closer.

The antennas and dishes had been rearranged into a more lenient design. It now looked more like an amalgamation of highly similar receiving dishes, but somehow wrong. The antennas were all either fully gone or changed into flat arrays that were clearly aligned to catch incoming waves of... of what, actually? The dishes were chaotically aligned around a half sphere. They now faced towards the nebula, not towards Earth. From what McKinney could understand, no part of this new contraption should be able to send or receive anything from Earth. He was not even sure if anything could send at all. However, it was clear that the receiving aspect had been enhanced significantly. He walked around the gigantic half-sphere of dishes to find some form of maintenance access. But there was none. Puzzled, he went back to the airlock. He knew that he had to report this. But he would have to think about what he had just seen before he could make any accurate remarks.

Suddenly, another beam of burning bright light purged the universe around him. The smiting brightness carved a path through the endless beauty of the nebula directly towards the Silent Prophet. He had learned and immediately ducked for cover, crawling the rest of the way to the hatch face down. Blinded partially by the residual brightness that was able to overcome his precautions, he forced his eyes shut. He held them tightly shut, straining his facial muscles into a painful cramp. He hastily felt around for the hatch grip.

There it was!

Shut the door! SHUT THE DOOR!

He slowly reopened his eyes. He could still see the brightness through the airtight cracks around the hatch. Then it stopped again. Suddenly, what used to be normal light seemed like impenetrable darkness. He sat down and awaited the decontamination gas to fill the room. His body sank to the floor. His mind wandering around the strange device that used to be the communication array.

-◇-

After exiting the airlock, Gonzales was already waiting for him. He was nervous. That much was obvious.

"Ian, we have a big problem!" Not the words McKinney had wanted to hear, but also not the words that really surprised him.

"What happened?" After speaking those words, McKinney felt how very tired he actually was. He had a headache. It must have been the strain from having been outside for so long. Maybe in combination with his completely exhausted eyes that were still not fully recovered.

"Wolf... she is gone." A slight crack in Gonzales's voice told McKinney more than the words he had spoken.

Wolf has vanished, and Gonzales was also reaching the limit of his professional external demeanor.

McKinney had been outside of his comfort zone for a long time, but seeing Gonzales wavering hit hard. He always used to be reliable and positive in situations that had already completely gone over McKinney's head. Not this time, it seemed. Not just different but seemingly impossible to fully understand. He didn't think less of Gonzales for showing cracks in his resilience. It was to be expected. However, he had hoped that things were different—hoped that someone would maintain stability.

"So... what now?" McKinney did not want to show his frustration, so he kept his words short. Adding more words would make him sound nervous, and this nervousness could affect Gonzales even further. McKinney's head was looping around its own logic. The pause that came as a result of the short answer would at least give McKinney a moment of respite.

Gonzales was silent for a bit. Then he said, "We should return."

"Return to where?" McKinney almost shouted. "Return home? To Earth? How?"

Gonzales looked at him. His eyes filled slowly with clarity of realization. Without proper maintenance and readable navigation, it would be a blind flight into the unknown. A single calculation error could throw them off in a completely wrong direction. Potentially catapulting them thousands of lightyears away from their target. The simple fact was: at the moment they had no means of calculating anything due to the unreadable output from all terminals.

Gonzales thought for a moment and then answered slowly: "We have to get away from that thing." He pointed at the ceiling toward the nebula. "At least we would be closer to Earth to be able to get help more quickly when we send out a distress signal."

Now McKinney felt ill in his stomach. That was a very valid plan. Or would have been if the comms still did what they had originally been designed for. Slowly he tried to motivate his words to leave his mouth. "We..." he swallowed hard "... we... we lost comms."

Gonzales's eyes fixated on McKinney. His face was made of stone, and no muscle moved.

"The comms array, Carlos..." McKinney added, "it's different now. It got... changed." McKinney tried to find the proper words to explain the situation. His mind was racing. Speaking few words would not work this time; he felt them bubble up. He had to let it all out.

"You see, all transmission antennas... they are gone - or changed. Changed to something different. Something that looks like the other receivers. Comms is now only receiving. Also, it was realigned. We no longer receive from earth, we receive from... well... from the nebula." McKinney somehow was unable to fully make sense of his own words. He had to laugh - not because it was funny, but because it was a reflex. A reflex of his frustration, his helplessness, his loss of hope and faith. He began to realize that they were stranded. Out here. With the nebula. The beautiful, wonderful nebula. The mother of the universe. His mother. He started to feel comfortable, homely, secure, watched over, taken care of. His laughter slowly became more joyful.

8. Shadows

McKinney had calmed himself down again. He had lost his composure, and that wasn't like him. He realized that this situation had derailed him further than even the death of his parents. Thinking back, he could see how the situation was dire. At first glance, perhaps it was even insurmountable. Fatalism did not help, but it tended to creep up in situations such as these. Now, back in the mess, he looked at Gonzales, who was sitting right next to him. McKinney felt a bit embarrassed to not be of better help to his old friend. After all, it had been Gonzales who had requested McKinney to join the expedition. Now McKinney felt as if he were just dead weight. Self-doubt had been a trusty companion for most of McKinney's life. A companion he really did not need or want anywhere near him, but who was always there for him when he needed him least. He averted his head and stared down at the sludge on his plate. Analyzing it closely as if it had a different color than usual—and maybe it did. Who knew what was what on this ship anymore? It was all as if reality did not function as expected anymore.

On the opposite side, Duong was sitting. Judging eyes attempted to make sure nobody looked in her direction for too long. Gonzales did seem to have is-sues with being judged. So he freely distributed his attention between the two.

"So you are sure what you saw was not an illusion, or a mistake, or something else?" Duong again de-manded that same answer from McKinney. He had al-ready lost count of how many times she had asked him. He wondered if she thought the same thing about the distorted symbols that had replaced all their let-ters.

"Yes, Duong, I am absolutely sure. I checked eve-rything as well as I could!" Again, he uttered the same answer.

"So are we stuck now?" Duong wanted to know.

"It seems so, Linh. Going anywhere now will be unpredictable. We need to plan our next move well," Gonzales sounded calm and collected, but McKinney could see the nervousness. The small cracks in his voice. The slight shaking of his leg. Gonzales played it cool, but he really wasn't. "For now, we need to find Wolf and understand what needs to be done." He added.

So they were already on a first-name basis. Old memories emerged in McKinney's mind. He tried to suppress them and focus on what was important now.

McKinney stabbed at his slime, trying to think of where anyone could hide on such a small ship. It was also well sealed off. No air ducts, no giant cargo hold - really no places to hide that he could think of. There wasn't even any door to close aside from the sanitary installations in the crew quarters and the crew doors. There wasn't even a bed to crawl under. It was factually impossible to hide on this ship for a longer time. Even actively avoiding everyone would be hard to accomplish. Everything on the ship was connected through one central corridor.

Standing up quickly, he muttered, "We should split up and comb the ship again." It was not a new idea. They had done that before without any luck, but he had to get active. He could not stand just sitting around doing nothing. With that, he left the room before anyone else could formulate a complete sentence.

-◇-

Her room is a mess! McKinney thought to himself as he stepped out. Behind him, the door slid out of the wall back into a closed position, hiding the piles of paper and strange markings on the wall Wolf had left behind. McKinney had never seen anything like it. It did not seem particularly sane. Yet, he thought that this could all be due to Wolf trying to understand what those strange symbols could mean. With everything going on, it seemed to be one of the more human notions. Almost explainable.

Deep in thought, he walked towards the bridge. Duong and Gonzales were searching the engineering bay at the back of the ship. As he passed the hop pod room, he felt it. Like a sudden movement in the air around him. An energy field, not too strong, but strong enough to pull him out of his thoughts. A shift within the ship. Something unnatural had occurred somewhere near him. A dreadful feeling overcame him. Had he just experienced the manipulation that had plagued the ship for the past weeks? He shivered, put his arms around himself to maintain some heat. Even though he knew that there could not be any real cold, he felt the air had cooled off significantly around him. As he continued towards the bridge, it immediately got warmer again. He reached back and could not feel any cold behind him. Whatever had happened, it was gone now. A better word that sprang to his mind to replace 'gone' was 'completed.' It was completed now.

Deep in thought, he barely noticed the hand on his shoulder that was trying to pull him back into reality.

"Hey Ian, everything ok with you?". Gonzales did always have a calming voice. It wasn't as calming as it used to be at the academy during tests, but it helped. Duong stood behind him with a slightly worried look on her face.

"Not sure, something happened here. I am not sure. I felt something," McKinney brought forward.

Gonzales's eyes moved down the corridor leading to the bridge. The door was now slightly open. A pale light cut through the opening in a straight line down the corridor. This wasn't good. Doors on the ship were controlled by motion sensors and always stayed closed. Doors should never remain open. Both McKinney and Gonzales stared at the gap in the door and understood. McKinney still felt weak in his knees and hesitated to move.

Gonzales was more forward. He looked at McKinney and commanded with a strong voice: "Let's find out."

He then held McKinney by the joint of his hand and dragged him toward the jarring door.

The feeling was gone, and McKinney still did not fully grasp what had happened. His mind raced around all the other technology that was on this ship, and he wondered how much of it had changed as well. Had this only been the door controls? That made no sense. The doors were opening anyway. Why would this need to change?

Slowly, McKinney felt stronger again. His legs started moving again, and he followed Gonzales with ease, matching his speed. Noticing this, Gonzales let go of McKinney's hand. Both men moved quickly down the corridor until they reached the door to the bridge. Duong came in right after them and took position in front of the door.

Without notice, the door opened completely and Wolf dashed through. She stopped and noticed her crew standing next to the door frame. Swiftly, she glanced over each of them. She seemed erratic yet focused. With a gaze cold and calculating, she looked at her crew for a moment. Then she turned to leave and noticed, "The hop back to Earth is initiated. You should get ready."

McKinney looked at Gonzales and found him staring right back at him. "Next hop home? When did

Wolf decide this?"

He looked back towards the bridge and noticed that the door to the bridge had now stayed open completely. Immediately, he realized that it was not the doors that were affected, but perhaps the ship's internal sensors. Bending forward slightly to get a quick peek into the bridge, he saw that the flight controls did not look the way he remembered them.

Before McKinney could inspect the situation any further, Gonzales had started pushing him and Duong toward the hop pod room.

As he got shoved back down the hall, McKinney was overcome by sadness. He realized he did not want to leave the nebula. He wanted to see more, get closer. He would never see the nebula again. He would lose it forever. Sadness deepened to dread that attempted to claim every fiber of his body. Then panic overcame him. He dropped to his knees. He could hear Wolf giving Gonzales orders, but his mind blended the words into a meaningless background noise. His thoughts were spinning around in his mind at a tremendous speed. He did not hear Gonzales scream at him. He did not feel Duong picking him up. He did not realize how he was put into his pod.

And then he was asleep.

He was in darkness. He felt the pull of the nebula stronger than ever. It reached out to him, offering him shelter and protection from the pain of separation. Again he was sitting on the warm, grass-covered ground. Around him a distortion became more and more visible as if another reality was forcing itself into his dream. Then, from the distortion, spawned thin, translucent tendrils, first only a few, then more and more. They appeared and disappeared again, moving and slithering chaotically around him. They wound themselves around his ankles and legs and held him in place. Around him the darkness made way for shapeless shapes appearing and disappearing as they seemed to invade his dream from a place beyond. McKinney felt as if he could make out forms sometimes. Something nearly humanoid. All appeared within misty clouds of indistinguishable shapes. But they were gone too quickly to grasp. Then they were pulled into a distorted background.

When he opened his eyes, he stared directly at it. A dark figure was hanging above his pod, suspended in mid-air by translucent tendrils. He saw no eyes, but he felt a stare from the void that was the shape. The more he tried to see, the less he actually saw. It was as if the light was being swallowed by a void emanating from the shadows. He had never felt so drained and empty. It was as if his very being was sucked out of him. He tried to look away. The few slivers of light still beaming through the room showed that Gonzales was moving and seemingly awake. His eyes wide open, his body shivering as shadows enshrouded his pod as well. It was too dark to see any of the other pods. Along with the eternal darkness that now flooded his vision came an unbearable silence. He then realized that a single sound became eerily audible close to his head. It sounded like the cold sparking of electricity screeching and scratching at his pod's outer shell. His eyes did not help. Through the darkness, he could not see what was happening. He felt it. He felt that something was forcing its way into his pod. Just like what had happened to Wolf. He could not move his head. The pod's safety measures restricted him. He tried to scream. He tried to free himself, but it was futile.

Then something pulled the darkness away. The scratching sound stopped. The room lit up. The jump was over. Where the shadows had just stood, there was no trance left. McKinney's pod opened, and he fell out. Immediately, he checked the large screen for passenger and flight information.

McKinney saw it immediately: The Silent Prophet has jumped closer to the Trapezium, not further away.

He felt happiness and smiled. As he turned around towards the rest of the pods, he froze in place. A look at the faces of his crewmates made him realize: they had all shared the experience—not a dream. This time, everyone had seen it happen. Seen the things, the shapeless shadows. Had felt the dread, the horror.

9. Patterns

"It was Wolf. She did this on purpose!" McKinney had never seen Gonzales so infuriated. Everyone was shaken, but Gonzales appeared to be especially angry. He had stretched out his arm, pointing at the captain.

She was not having it: "Careful, first officer. Don't forget who you are talking to. I made a decision and set the course. I am certain I set the course toward Earth!"

"Then why are we closer to the nebula—AGAIN!" Gonzales screamed.

"You will fall in place, First Officer. I am still the captain of this ship." Wolf's demeanor was almost calm on the surface, but it was easy to hear the small jitters signaling the storm brewing underneath the surface. McKinney had never heard Wolf pull rank on anyone—but then again, he had never heard anyone attack her like Gonzales had done.

Gonzales stared daggers at Wolf for a moment, then stepped back. Wolf remained standing in her place. Deeply leaning into her position of clear superiority. The messy room, the absence, the clear signs of instability she had shown earlier, none of that seemed to matter anymore. McKinney would not take sides against her and knew that Duong would see it the same way. Yes, there were strange occurrences. But until now, there had never been anything that would question her capability as captain. Her posture was straight and her voice was clear. She looked at everyone in the room as if she wanted to challenge them to oppose her. Finally, her eyes targeted McKinney. He had tried to not be part of the turmoil. Wolf's hardened stare snapped him out of his thoughts. He immediately wished himself far away from what was happening here at that moment. After a short while, she shook her head and her gaze became more leveled again.

"Well, we all have work to do. Let's get to it. No need to waste more time. You all know the drill." Back to her normal voice, the tension seemed gone. However, the commanding tone was still a bit more strict than usual.

Unsurprisingly, Gonzales got up first and left the room. Clearly, he needed to vent his anger. McKinney felt it would be best to leave his friend alone. He had something better to do: he was going to go out first to check the comms array again. He was happy about that—or rather, relieved. He was not torn away from the warm, motherly embrace of the Trapezium.

Already upon leaving the pod room, McKinney realized that this ship was most certainly not the same one he had seen before the hop. Somehow, the ship had been warped ever so slightly. He could not put his finger on it. It seemed as if the ripple effects that he had previously seen wherever the changes had occurred were now to be found in many areas of the ship.

Arriving at the airlock, he noticed that the casing where the suits were on also had such ripple effects. This gave him an uneasy feeling. The suits had to remain airtight. Any structural change could have devastating effects. His trust in the material went down. However, he really wanted to get out. To see the Trapezium, to feel the embrace. He took one of the suits for closer inspection. It had distortions here and there on the material, but none of them seemed to have caused any openings. At first glance, the suit seemed unchanged despite clearly being affected. McKinney needed a few moments to accurately pinpoint the differences. The neck collar was made up of a steel frame embedded into the lighter aluminum casing. This was then sewn and glued into the suit - or at least, it should have been. Now it seemed as though the three materials had been fused together into a single restructured alloy that did not at all feel natural to the touch. It still had the required strength at the connection point to the helmet. Just below that, it became softer for the more mobile requirements of the shoulder and arms' movement. It also felt extremely cold in McKinney's hands as he slowly caressed the strange amalgamation of materials. As he put on the suit, he could not help but notice the soft pulsating vibration resonating from within the fabric. As if it were still shifting on its own. What had changed for the ship to feel so - alive?

McKinney decided to take the risk. The suit felt

solid. After attaching the helmet, air flooded in and it felt as it should. Maybe even a bit lighter around the neck. He was deeply curious to see if the comms array had further transformed since the last inspection. In reality, he knew he wanted to go out, see, and embrace the nebula once more.

Eagerness and anticipation spread through his body. It coursed through his veins and numbed his mind as the airlock slowly cycled. He did not even care anymore that his suit was now a fused construct. It was fluctuating in integrity and material strength whenever he set himself in motion. He only cared for what awaited him outside: the endless beauty of the nebula. Its shining colors enveloping every thought in his mind and wrapping themselves around every fiber of his being. He was so much closer to his destiny— now that it was all around him. He could not touch it, but the black void of space behind him was now gone. Wherever he looked, he only saw the beauty of the fire of creation.

He paused and noticed that the nebula should not look like this. The particles were supposed to be so far apart that the nebula itself was nothing but a faint, diffused glow when looking at it from this close. Yet somehow, his mind had expected this view. It felt normal to him.

Curiosity helped to tear his mind loose from the soothing thought of staying in that one place forever. All he had ever wanted was to stare at the divine beauty of the colorful clouds and the shifting constellation of the Trapezium. It was another sharp ray of radiant light cutting violently through the landscape of colorful clouds that made him regain focus. He concentrated again on the task at hand.

McKinney scrambled across the ship's outer hull and made his way toward the comms array. He had very little concept of how to prepare himself for whatever might await him there. Up until now, the changes that had happened on the unit had increased exponentially in intensity. He could feel the excitement swelling up in him as his eyes fell on what was once their lifeline home. What he saw could not have been further away from what he had expected to see. The generally technical shape had hardly changed. Yet the whole structure was now engulfed in some sort of shifting energy shield. He could hardly make out the actual shape of the comms array. The field around it seemed to be in constant flux, showing and hiding its contents in chaotic frequency. The shape within seemed unreal. It appeared to be very static but at the same time it looked different at every moment. It seemed as if it were constantly changing without signaling the change.

McKinney recognized what he was looking at. He had seen this construct before - in his dreams. It was not this intense, but the "irreality" of the concept had been there whenever the strange darkness had invaded his dreams. He was very uncertain about how to approach the situation. A part of him wanted to touch the surface of the field. It felt unnecessarily dangerous.

What if his hand were subject to these strange changes as well? He tried to cool down his head and think the situation through.

Slowly, McKinney got closer to the structure. He wondered if there would be any discernible label or readout that would help to explain what exactly his eyes were seeing. However, looking at them would require at least some contact with the strange field that was surrounding the construct. Slowly, he reached out his hand, targeting a space where the inner structure seemed closest to the field. As his hand got near, the field seemed to react and started warping towards his fingers as if being attracted to them. He stopped for a second and thought about pulling back his hand. But something kept him going. Then, his hand finally made contact with the field. He felt a tingling. A cold breeze passed through the suit and made him shiver. The field seemed not to affect him. However, he did not want to push his luck further than necessary and decided to move fast. Using his fingers only, he felt for the surface of the construction. It was always somewhat in fluctuation. That made him realize that the actual distance of the object from him was nearly impossible to understand. Suddenly, he felt something solid. He moved his hand along its surface and noticed how inconsistent the surface was with the information his eyes were given. Sometimes, his hands were clearly far away from the object, yet he felt it. Then, other times, his hand should have been inside the object, yet he could barely reach it. It fascinated him, but it did not help him understand what was actually going on. After a short while, he decided to stop his efforts. Slowly, he pulled back his hand, hoping it was not affected by the distortion field.

As he continued to pull back, he noticed that it had become more and more difficult. Something was holding him. He sped up his movement, but the harder he pulled, the more it pulled him in. Suddenly he lost footing. In icy shiver crept up and down his spine as his full body got absorbed in the distortion field. He struggled to get back on his feet. Countless images flooded his mind. His skin felt as if it were being pulled and pressed in all directions. He fought against the pain as the intensity slowly increased. All the while his mind was being assaulted with distorted impressions he could not sort out. Desperately grappling for the safety lanyard, his hands finally found purchase. He pulled with all the strength he could muster. For a while he thought the more he pulled, the deeper he went into the field. New images shot through his mind. Landscapes, shadow beings, something large. All was chaotic and impossible to comprehend. He felt as if the steel rope was becoming more and more loose in his hands. Somehow reality was not functioning in his field. He tried to ignore it. He instinctively knew that outside the field reality must still be in check and whatever he felt and experienced in here was limited to this space. His head hurt and his mind was about to break under all the information imprinting itself. It was impossible to focus on his task.

Muscle memory and desperation pushed him on. He kept pulling and inching his way forward.

Abruptly, the field let go of him and he tumbled out, hanging freely in space for a few moments. The pain had stopped. The images had stopped. Drops of blood floated in his helmet. His mind was still spinning from all the information. He took a moment to sort his thoughts before he slowly reeled himself back to the deck.

-◇-

As McKinney stepped back onto the bridge, he was greeted by the whole crew standing around the conference table at the back of the room. The door had been open and did not close behind him. He was late. He took his time to fully analyze his body for any changes. His skin was rippled in many places, and when taking off the suit, some parts had started to fuse with his skin. It had been painful, and on a few occasions, he had lost a bit of skin. Nothing a few band-aids could not fix. McKinney had decided not to inform the others. He did not need help, and they would only question him again about his supposed addiction to the nebula. They could never understand what had happened anyway. He was too busy and didn't need additional nonsense to discuss.

As McKinney drew closer to the group, he realized that the tension in the room was a lot higher than what he had left behind.

"Is there a new problem?" His question was almost irrelevant to him because he knew there had to be a bigger problem still. He also knew that the further they moved on, the worse things would become.

"It is the readouts, Ian... it has gotten worse again - a lot worse." Gonzales's voice sounded dry and monotone. Something in him had given up.

McKinney took his place at the table and looked at the screens and readouts presented. It was a mess at first sight. The symbols were no longer identifiable as such. It looked more like an amalgamation of lines and curves covering the pages. He could also see the same distortion effect that he had seen on the comms array. When not trying to follow a line on the paper, it seemed not to go where he expected it to go when he first saw the page. It felt as if reality did not apply to the documents. A constant chaotic shift ran through everything. Yet the longer he stared at it, the more he started to get the feeling that he knew what was written on the paper. No words. Instead, a seemingly meaningful pattern started to emerge in his mind. He could not make out what that meaning was. But he started to feel dizzy from looking at the endless amounts of structure covering the screens and pieces of paper on the table. He shook his head and looked around.

He noticed Wolf. Her eyes focused, her mind obviously absent. Her demeanor was a wordless but clear communication. Somehow, McKinney fully understood what was going on in her mind. McKinney did not want to disturb her thoughts, but he noticed that Gonzales might make that attempt. Something was tugging at his mind to hold him back. So he decided to maintain his composure and let things play out.

"Wolf, what do you see?" a soft attempt it was. Quite in contradiction to his earlier outburst and ultimately meaningless. Wolf did not react at first. Then, after a good long moment of silence, she turned her head and stared him dead in the eyes.

"I see a pattern." Words slowly left her mouth. Indeed, McKinney understood what Wolf was saying between the lines all too well. This was not nonsense as before. This was very much a proper communication, just not one he could yet understand.

With a quick hand, she swiped the paper pile away from the table and moved toward the door.

"I will investigate this further on my own time!" With these quick last words, she exited.

Some sort of jealousy arose in McKinney. He did not know why and could not understand the rationale behind his feelings. But for some reason, he really wanted to have those readouts back. He wanted to understand them before anyone else.

McKinney looked back at the others and saw that everyone was bewildered, but no one seemed to have a wish to follow Wolf. At least not overbearingly enough to show it. In fact, Gonzales even looked much less concerned than he should have. Almost as if he had been expecting this behavior, but he also looked resigned and tired. McKinney approached him and put his hand on the shoulder of his old friend.

"Hey Carlos, are you okay?"

"Yes, Ian. I just have not slept well for a while." Gonzales's voice sounded tired and frustrated. McKinney had a hunch about how Gonzales must feel. He was usually in control of all situations, and now it was all slipping out from under his hands. He had lost traction. He had lost control.

For a while, the two friends looked at each other in silence. Then Gonzales smiled a little. Some things were still right. If things got this bad, both of them knew they could ultimately rely on one another.

"Go to bed, get some rest!" McKinney said. Gonzales nodded, tired, and slowly left the room.

Duong has been leaning against a wall to the side, eyeing the situation curiously. As McKinney turned to her, he caught her intense stare.

"What happened to you?" she asked McKinney.

"I... nothing!" McKinney replied, slightly taken aback.

"You are hurt. Go to the infirmary." She pushed herself away from the wall slowly, always maintaining eye contact. After a while, she moved swiftly past McKinney and silently left the room.

How did she know this? What is going on in her mind? McKinney was puzzled by her reaction, but even more puzzled by his own reply. Why did he feel the need to hide from her that he might have been killed only a few minutes ago?

10. Confrontation

Walking down the corridor was a lot more complicated than Gonzales had remembered for some reason. His legs would not obey his mind. He shifted from wall to wall, slowly drifting towards his room. He had difficulty forming a single thought. It was not just the general exhaustion. There was more. He felt his whole world was spinning out of control. Whatever had happened to Wolf, it still puzzled him. He had issues trusting her now. Where had she been, and what had she been up to in her time of absence? Who could he still fully trust? McKinney had also acted strangely. Duong was the only person who seemed to have been unaffected, but maybe she was just good at hiding it. Was it perhaps he himself who was going insane?

Finally, he had reached the door of his quarters. It opened, and for some reason, it closed behind him again. He barely noticed that the doors no longer closed automatically except for his own. All he could really think about was his bed. Not even bothering to take off his clothes, he dropped onto his mattress. He could not remember his last thoughts as his eyes shut and he fell into a deep sleep.

-◇-

When he woke up, his room was drenched in complete darkness. Gonzales had no idea how long he had slept, but it must have been hours at least when he was awakened by a cold breeze blowing over him. His hands felt for the light switch that was forged into the wall. Yet, his fingers touched nothing but the cold steel that made up the walls of his room. He strained his eyes in the dark to make out rough shapes around him. Upon turning around, he noticed that the light switch was no longer where it should be. His hands grappled around in the dark. Somehow, his room was different. The bed was now lodged between the side walls of the room, and the space next to the bed. It was normally used for a nightstand on either side. Now these had fused into the walls. His hands told him that basic shapes were still somewhat traceable in the walls. One of them was the lamp. Searching further, he finally found the switch. Hoping that the wiring was still intact, he pressed it. A pale light emanated from the wall. The light was working, but nowhere close to its complete potential. Still, he could at last make out more than basic shapes. His eyes tried to figure out what had happened to his room. It looked as though the formerly distinct artifacts of his room had now merged. Materials were molded together, and everything seemed to be in constant fluctuation. A distortion rippled through most of his room. The light itself seemed to be inside the wall. Yet, he could still move the lamp itself around relatively freely. It was difficult to tell how much of the lamp was inside the wall. A very slight discrepancy between what his fingers felt and what his eyes told him made estimates necessary.

The dim light of the lamp was able to outline about half of the room. The far wall harboring the door was still drenched in complete and impenetrable darkness. There was a light switch next to the door for operating the ceiling light. He hoped it was still functional and not already fused with something else as well. He noticed that the light did not really fade away as much as it just stopped in the middle of the room. It looked as if something was blocking it.

He shifted the lamp towards the center of the room. He froze and his heart almost skipped a beat. Something was there. He could barely make out a silhouette of something standing in his room. He tried to get a handle on himself for a second and struggled out of his bed. Carefully, he got closer. He saw a somewhat familiar silhouette. Slender, small, feminine. A silhouette that looked like... Duong. Relief and happiness filled his mind. He had felt an attraction to Duong ever since they had been introduced. The more of a cold shoulder he had gotten from her, the more his hunting instinct had been triggered. Eventually, she had started to warm up to him. His old tricks had never failed him and now, was this finally the moment he had been working towards? But something wasn't right.

"Linh?" he asked softly.

Movement.

Silence.

Slowly, the silhouette stepped forward into the dim light of the lamp. But whenever it took a step closer and Gonzales expected the light to finally brighten the dark figure, the light seemed to grow ever dimmer. The figure would not be unraveled from its dark cloak.

This was not Duong.

Gonzales slid back onto his bed, toward the only light source in his room. He fumbled around with the lamp to shift it further in the direction of the being.

... and then he finally realized it was close enough. But what he saw was not the warm and beautiful body of Duong. Instead, he only saw a dark towering figure looming above him. Ever-moving and shifting tendrils extended in all directions. Their ends appeared and vanished into small fields of distortion. The tendrils were keeping the figure suspended in midair. The creature's presence seemed to swallow all light. In terror, he could not scream. Air would not leave his lungs. Desperately, he closed his eyes. He knew, if he stared longer, there would be no return. He could feel its thoughts invading his mind. Messages raced by. He could not make sense of them. He saw images of a place of complete chaos and impossible reality. He saw images of dark beings worshiping an unseen force. He saw so many things he could not understand. The amount of information racing through his mind caused unbelievable agony.

But then finally, like a beacon in the endless darkness, a single thought appeared in his mind. He focused all his efforts on capturing it. Holding onto it. A simple thought that only contained a single important message. It said: "scream."

And he screamed. He screamed as loud and as long as he could. It was a hollow scream of pain and horror. A scream that contained all the power of a man fearing for his life. He screamed until his vocal cords distorted into an ugly screech. And the screech finally turned into a croaking sound, reminiscent of a dying raven's last breath.

The door slid open with an uncaring soft hiss, and McKinney fell into the room. Light flooded from the ceiling and cleansed the room of darkness and pain.

Gonzales opened his eyes. The void that had surrounded him was gone. All that was left was McKinney's stare and his hurting throat.

McKinney stayed with his old friend for a while. Gonzales needed time to recover. His throat hurt, and his mind was spinning. Other than that, he felt fine. Exhausted but fine.

"I think you have more gray hair, old man," McKinney noticed jokingly. The joke passed by Gonzales. It did not surprise him if that were true after his encounter.

11. Ancient

Throughout her career, Wolf had always been far above average at solving problems. She instinctively knew when there was something out of the ordinary. An anomaly, a pattern. Her instincts had not once deceived her. Therefore, her will to find what she was missing had remained unbroken. She had dug deep through mountains of data sheets and heaps of paper that were piling up all around her room. But the message stayed hidden. There had to be a pattern. There had to be something she had overlooked. Wolf hoped that the new evidence would help clarify.

She had again forgotten time and space around her. Laser-focused on this issue. Captivated by what she had at hand - just like last time. Her door was locked and nobody had dared to knock. Maybe her crew got used to it. She had already wondered what had happened last time. She never remembered anyone trying to contact her. When they told her that she hadn't been in her room, she did not know what to believe. Of course she had been there. Where else should she have been? In her dream? What nonsense!

Her body told her to stop, eat, and drink, but her mind would not allow her to. However, she was starting to reach the limitations of her physical capabilities. Her eyes grew weary, her muscles grew tired, and she could barely keep up anymore. Her focus started to fade away—and then her vision grew blurry. All the while, her brain was screaming desperately for her to continue. She tried. She felt a dire need for a solution.

But she drifted away. The room was parting below her. She was falling into endless darkness. Free-floating in space. Slowly, shapes appeared around her. At first, the shapes made no sense. Gradually, they started warping and twisting into different shapes. The shapes started twirling and fluctuating into patterns, and images started to appear. The images were unclear, surreal. Wolf attempted to interpret what she saw. A place that could not be. A God. Confusion. A journey. A prison. Eons passed her by, it seemed. She witnessed stars being born and galaxies being destroyed. Her mind was tasked to withstand the knowledge of countless lives and the pain of countless deaths.

Her mind struggled to hold on to single thoughts. She tried to focus on memorizing just singular impressions. This already proved too much for her mind. She felt how her sanity was slowly being cracked into pieces like a porcelain vase being crushed under a rock. She was getting what she had wished for. The pattern unraveled in front of her very eyes. It contained information leading back uncountable eons. A greater truth far beyond human comprehension. Wolf realized with endless sorrow that she could never hope to understand the message. She could not find what it was that these images were trying to show her. All she knew was that it was the single most important message ever to be delivered to mankind. The images faded from her eyes and from her mind like an after-image of a dream.

Desperation overcame her. She searched her memory for anything to cling to. She tried recombining what she knew to build bridges in her head. But it was all for nothing. Her consciousness returned slowly. She opened her eyes and found herself back in her room, lying on the floor surrounded by piles of paper. All that remained was a single word.

With a weak voice, she let it escape her lips: "Zor'Xuuth."

Then she noticed that she was not alone in her room. A figure was standing in the far dark corner. Its very being seemingly swallowed all the light that wanted to touch it. She stared into a black void. Then everything went black.

12. Madness

McKinney had not seen Wolf for more than three days. In fact, no one had seen her since she left the bridge with the documents. The only thing they knew was that she had locked herself in her room. Without food, without water. Something was wrong. Knocking on the door did not help. Calling out to her did not help. She simply did not answer. And the crew became more and more worried about her well-being.

The last time she had vanished, she had not been in her room, but the door was unlocked. This time, the door was locked from the inside. It was not possible for her to be anywhere else.

It was on the 4th day after her disappearance. The crew sat together in the mess hall and decided they had to open the door to Wolf's room. Opening the door was no easy task. McKinney's first idea had, of course, been to use the central lock on the bridge. He had quickly realized that as the door automation was now unpowered, the central system was also powerless to open or close anything. It could not simply be pried open. Heavy-duty hydraulics were holding the doors shut as a safety measure. These would never be overpowered by a human hand no matter what tools it bore. Breaking it from the outside would be a futile attempt. The doors were made to withstand any sudden fall of pressure and exposure to the cold reality of space to protect whatever was on the other side. It would need a much more powerful force to give way than a few hands manually smashing into it with whatever hard objects they could find. Given the length of the trip, the security and safety of each sector of the Silent Prophet had been a concern in building the vessel. This was especially true for the crew quarters. What they needed was a mixture of methods.

"You are insane, McKinney!" Duong's words were emotionless but sharp.

"We don't really have a choice if we want to get in there." McKinney had a more than insane plan.

"You could kill her if this goes wrong." Duong was worried. Gonzales was quiet. His head was still spinning slightly from his encounter, and he felt ashamed looking at Duong.

"We have time, a few minutes at least. If we puncture the hydraulic pumps in the walls by the door frame, we can create a vacuum. The escaping hydraulic fluid will blow the door mechanism out of the wall. We can get her out and have her in safety in less than a minute." McKinney listened to himself talk and felt that Duong was right. He was insane, and he had not thought anything through. His head was filled with the image of Gonzales sitting on the floor of his room surrounded by a looming darkness. It immediately filled McKinney with dread deeper than he could bear at the moment. If the same thing had happened to Wolf, then he had to get in there. He had to see what happened.

For a while, there was nothing but silence. Nobody wanted to make the call. Finally, Duong got up.

"Everyone here has gone insane." She went for the door and stopped. Without turning around, she added, "Are you guys coming, or what?"

McKinney looked at Gonzales, puzzled. Then both men stood up and followed Duong out of the mess hall.

They had sealed off the crew quarters. Each of them went to their room to ensure the doors were open far enough for the air to escape swiftly and to stow away any loose items. The doors should hold, but the pressure would not be kind to any concealed pockets of air. They had to work fast. Some collateral damage would have to be accepted to save their captain. Duong rushed out of the area, and McKinney also felt that speed was of the utmost importance.

The bulkheads were controlled by the ship's computer but could also be drawn shut manually if needed. In current times, a manual approach would have to do. McKinney and Gonzales put on their pressurized suits. They had an extra suit with them, although they were unsure if it would even be possible to get an unconscious person into such a suit. It was a plan B in case plan A failed. Duong stayed behind at the controls next to the pressure door that was the entrance to the crew quarters. She would initiate the pressurization process again from there.

Using crowbars and cutters from engineering, McKinney got to work to remove the door frame. He noticed that some of it had fused together, making it necessary to cut through the thick steel. This would cost time. Time they probably did not have. The cutters worked fast and efficiently, and with some patience, the first part of the frame was removed and the hydraulic system was laid bare. One side of the double sliding door would be enough. It would be impossible to fully cut the pumps apart. Yet, that was not necessary. A hole big enough for liquid to escape would be all they needed. The sudden vacuum would do the rest. And rip out the liquid, the pump, and everything attached to it—hopefully.

McKinney looked at Gonzales and nodded. There was no turning back now. McKinney pushed the cutter into the back end of each of the three hydraulic pumps. A fizzling sound was audible even through the helmet whenever the plasma blade punctured deep enough to touch the liquid inside.

It was finally done. Now the rest of the plan was simple. McKinney would trigger the fire suppression system, which creates a vacuum in that section after two minutes. The expectation was that this was enough power to blow Wolf's door right out of its frame. A slight problem would be that the section would also turn off the gravitational buffers. After that, Duong would unset the alarm state and reinitialize the atmospheric pressure in the crew quarters. The whole process should hopefully take less than six minutes in total.

"We are really doing this, I guess." McKinney wasn't so sure of his plan anymore. He knew the ship inside out, but in such a rush, he was also sure that he would forget something important.

"Your idea, McKinney!" The headphones sounded slightly metallic in his ears. Duong knew how to make these two words feel like a painful scolding.

He turned his head toward her. She stood across the room at the far end next to the sealed pressure door at the entrance, one hand on a safety handle and one hand on the controls.

Slowly, McKinney started working on the fire sensor in the ceiling. It was fairly easy to trigger these once the basic mechanism behind the fire control system was understood. It only took a few seconds to dismantle the sensor's casing and then just a few more to bridge the alarm wire. A loud siren let him know that he had been successful.

Now the clock was ticking. The two minutes started stretching to an eternity. McKinney was just beginning to wonder if anything would happen. The siren was bursting out of his eardrums despite him wearing an airtight helmet. Suddenly, the screams of the siren were replaced by an aggressive suction noise. Then the gravitational buffers stopped. He slowly lost all sense of weight as he got lifted off the floor. He felt his suit react to the change in pressure and maneuverability. It was the exact same feeling he had when spacewalking. In less than a moment, it was all over, and the room was silent.

The door was still in its place. Unmoving, unwavering.

"Impossible!" Gonzales's words echoed in everyone's heads.

Then a vibration went through the walls, floor, and ceiling. Something was happening. The vacuum was absolute. Sound struggled to travel. Suddenly, the massive door was torn off its hinges in a violent release of pressure. It accelerated into the opposite wall. The enormous power of the impact bent and cracked the thick protective steel plates that separated the crew quarters from the inner corridor. A tremendous air explosion was set free that McKinney could not just feel but also hear very clearly. Hundreds of papers, items, and pieces of equipment followed in the wake of the air explosion and flew chaotically through the whole room. He lost his footing fast as he was thrown around the room like a children's toy. Finally, he hit a wall and only heard muffled sounds overridden by a strong tinnitus.

"Duong, now!" he screamed into the mic of his helmet without knowing how loud he was screaming or if anyone could actually hear him. "Start now!"

He noticed that Gonzales was already on his feet, making his way towards the now open room. All the pieces of paper with the nonsensical scribbles on them had taken away McKinney's clear vision. Working a path through the paper curtains, he was finally able to look into the room. He saw Wolf unconscious, slightly levitating above the floor, moving towards him. All around her were the pieces of paper with ink scribbles on them. They were flying wildly around the scene, disturbed by the sudden depressurization. Most had black ink, but some had red ink... no, not ink... that was blood.

"Oh my God, what has happened here?" Gonzales looked at him. He had noticed it too.

"It does not matter. We have to get her out of here!" McKinney wanted to act. His ears were still ringing, and he felt numb.

As he moved forward, a second tremendous blow of air pressure tore him off his feet. Right next to him, the second door of the double sliding doors was propelled with enormous force through the vacuum towards McKinney. McKinney had hoped that this would not happen, but the door frame was damaged enough to destabilize the complete construction. It caught hold of his arm as it bolted past him. Excruciating pain rushed through his nerves. The sudden impact sent him spinning through the vacuum until he smashed against the opposite wall. He struggled to stay conscious and managed to maintain blurry vision. His arm felt numb. His ears were ringing. A massive headache was starting to manifest itself. He decided to fight through it and struggled to his feet.

Then he saw it. A figure fully cloaked in absolute darkness. It slowly floated towards him. McKinney closed his eyes and shook his head. He felt that the pressure was returning to the cabin. Suddenly he started to hear voices again through his headphones. Distant and barely audible.

Then he felt Gonzales's hands pull him to the side. He looked up and saw his face full of fear. What was he afraid of? McKinney started to panic: his suit... was it damaged? He looked down to check his arm, but the suit seemed fine save for a few superficial scratches. The nano-fiber fabric was designed to withstand a lot of punishment. McKinney's arm, however, was not. The rising pressure on the suit caused further discomfort. The starting gravitational buffers pulled on his arm and his head. McKinney winced.

Then he looked back up and noticed that Gonzales did not look at him. Instead, he looked in the direction McKinney had seen the figure. He looked but saw nothing. The shape he had seen before had vanished completely. Instead, he now saw Wolf again. Laying on the floor. Her fingers were bleeding, and blood had streamed from her eyes and ears. McKinney made his way towards Wolf and saw that Gonzales had already reached her.

"Wolf!" Gonzales had found his clear priorities. McKinney helped Gonzales as best he could with his healthy arm to carry her to the pressure door. Doung was already working on getting it open.

13. Aggression

"Please hold still, Ian!" Gonzales was getting frustrated. He had checked McKinney's arm and told him about all the wonderful colors McKinney would be seeing on his arm in the next few weeks. But he could assure him that nothing was broken. Some ice spray had already helped a lot. McKinney was back in action and moving erratically through the med bay. Gonzales tried to keep up with him to put a cooling bandage on his shoulder to better support his arm.

Duong was standing in front of him with an empty, tired stare. But she was soldierly enough to maintain a certain stance. McKinney was sure she had shut down internally. No sensible words would come out of her, so he instead talked to Gonzales.

"It all worked, Carlos - well, sort of, but we achieved what we wanted, right? How is Wolf? Should we investigate her room?" He was breathless.

The opening of Wolf's door excited him. There was a lot to unravel, and his head was spinning in all directions. He wanted to go back and check the papers. He wanted to know what happened to Wolf. His shoulder hurt, and he wanted to lie down and rest, ideally all at the same time.

Gonzales had caught up to him and was wrapping McKinney's shoulder while he answered, "I have not yet checked on Wolf. First your shoulder, and then I will see to her. She is stabilized for now, but she is still unconscious. What else did you ask?"

McKinney had forgotten it himself. No matter, his first goal was to get his hands on whatever Wolf had been working on.

"Did you notice that her hair has turned even whiter?" McKinney asked.

"I have not yet checked." Gonzales had seen it as well, but before he had really understood the situation, he did not want to comment on it. "There, all done. You will not be able to play basketball with that arm, but at least the pain should be bearable." Gonzales went to a drawer and picked out a box with an unreadable name on it. The image on the box was also distorted, but its original shape could still be guessed. He passed the box to McKinney. "Here, take 2 whenever the pain gets too bad."

McKinney took the box of pills and immediately opened it, putting two pills in his mouth.

"I have to check Wolf's room now." He spoke and went for the door.

To his surprise, Duong followed him. She did not speak and seemed far away in her thoughts. As they went down the corridor, McKinney started feeling awkward about the situation. Striking up some small talk sounded like a relieving idea in his head.

"So, you look tired." He said in a neutral tone.

Duong did not answer right away, but she lifted her head and looked at him. After an uncomfortable while she finally said: "McKinney... can I show you something?"

Looking at the aftermath of the rescue allowed McKinney more insight into what his plan had actually done to the ship. The anteroom before the separate crew rooms was in complete disarray. The steel plating was ripped open across the full length of the wall. Next to Wolf was Gonzales's door. It was completely damaged. McKinney had no idea how Gonzales would be able to ever get into his room again. At least without fully cutting away the mashed-together parts of the door and door frame. Duong's door was also no longer fully on its hinges, and the frame was torn apart, with one part hanging on less than two rivets and the rest bent far outward.

Duong took a piece of steel that was lying on the floor and used it as a makeshift crowbar to manually open her door. After a couple of tries, she managed to slip it between the two door parts. With a nod, she requested McKinney to help her pull. It took a lot of strength and willpower to pry apart the two sides of the door and create a gap big enough for McKinney to pass through. The material was screeching as wedged steel plates scraped against each other and gave way. Finally, the path was open, and McKinney followed Duong into her room.

The room was in bad shape. The inner wall was also damaged, and cables were sticking out of the walls no longer properly in their ducts. However, the light switch itself seemed to work well enough. As Duong swiped her hand over the sensor, the room illuminated. The former darkness was chased away in seconds.

Except it wasn't chased away completely.

In the corner next to the bed, darkness seemed to have collected that the light could not penetrate. Upon closer inspection, it became clear to McKinney that it was no ordinary shadow caused by the furniture. It had a shape, but McKinney had difficulty making it out. It was like staring into a void. Lights seemed to have little to no effect on whatever was lying in that corner. It didn't even seem to really be part of this reality.

McKinney stood close to the figure, staring at it in disbelief. "What... what is that?"

"I don't know..." Duong answered.

"Well... how did it get here?" McKinney was now looking at her. Expecting more of an answer this time.

"I was about to go to sleep, and it suddenly stood in my room." Duong paused. "No, he didn't stand, he floated... or... hung... or something like that."

McKinney started to shape an image in his head. He knew what she had encountered. Still, he had not yet seen one this close.

"I don't know how it got in," Duong continued, "I didn't even see it at first."

McKinney already knew fairly well what was going on. He was curious. How do you see something that dark in the darkness? "How did you notice it?"

"Soldier instinct?" Duong was lingering on that for a bit. "I honestly don't know. It made no sound, but I felt its presence, and then I saw movement in the dark."

Tendrils.

"Some... little ropes or something like that. Moving around... that," Duong pointed at the shapeless shape emanating pure darkness. "They were all around its body. Constantly moving. I could not see what they were attached to, but it looked as if they were holding it in some way."

"... suspended in the air?"

"Yes... I would even say tethered."

McKinney had to think about that one. Putting together the pieces, it seemed to fit. The tendrils seemed to be pulling at whatever was inside. Maybe they did not naturally belong to it?

"What do you think the tether connects to?" McKinney asked.

"You want my honest opinion?" Duong turned to him and looked him straight in the eye.

McKinney nodded. He had his own thoughts and wanted to match them to what Duong was thinking.

"They connect to something that is not... here," Duong struggled with the right words. "Not here with us, in this... space."

"Dimension?" McKinney asked.

"That sounds ridiculous, McKinney... but yes... something like that, I guess." She was now speaking slowly, almost carefully. "I honestly don't know. I saw some of the ropes or tendrils connect. They lead into some form of distortion, as if leading into nothingness. It felt as if they would continue endlessly, and yet end right there."

The impossibility of understanding a shape or a structure was something McKinney understood all too well. His moment in the distortion field of the former comms array showed it to him firsthand.

"I saw them disappear; why is it still here?"

"I think I killed it." Duong's voice was not showing any certainty. "It got close. I saw the tendrils reaching out for me. So I pulled my knife and started slashing."

"So you simply stabbed it?" McKinney was surprised that these things could be killed so easily.

"No. I did not stab at anything. I felt nearly no resistance, more a weird cold breeze whenever the blade should have found flesh." She put her hand into the dark void and pulled out a combat knife that had been sticking in the shadow. It had a long, clean blade. "On my blade, there was also nothing, no residue or anything, yet..." She gave McKinney the knife, and he noticed that it seemed malformed in subtle ways. "The contact changed the blade itself."

Stunned, McKinney stared at the blade. Even while looking at it, it still seemed to be in flux. Ever-changing and restructuring must be happening on an atomic level. He saw slight, barely visible shifts and distortions on the blade itself. He found it difficult to understand the construct he was holding in its exact form.

Yet he also wondered if prolonged exposure to an object like this would cause it to 'infect' him as well.

Giving the knife back to Duong, he said, "But then why did it not vanish this time, and where are the tethers?"

"Well, after slashing at it many, many times, the tendrils seemed to unravel, and the thing just dropped on my floor. It has been here ever since." Duong pointed at the black void in the corner next to the bed. McKinney was unsure, but he thought he saw movement in the shadow. "I think I might have disrupted the tethering somehow, and the shadow can't operate without it."

"Did you try to move it?"

"I tried; it is not really possible to get a hold of it. I don't know how to describe it." She thought for a moment about her words. McKinney had the feeling that something was happening in the dark shadow. Whenever he looked at it, he could not see anything but darkness.

Duong added: "I cannot understand its outline. And when I tried moving it with my foot, it seemed impossibly heavy and at the same time not really tangible."

McKinney was thinking again of the comms array. He knew exactly what she was talking about.

"I left the knife in there in hopes of pinning it down or something. The blade made the tethers vanish as best as I could deduce. So perhaps it could make the shadow stay so we can examine it," Duong said.

McKinney found no flaw in her logic. Maybe it was

the steel the knife was made of, maybe the movement, maybe something had been severed. It was impossible to say. "Yeah, maybe you should put it back."

As Duong wanted to kneel down, the room filled with an icy wind. Suddenly around the shadow, multiple smaller distortion fields appeared. Tendrils shot out, enshrouding the shadow in fractions of a second. Slowly the shapeless form took shape again. Almost humanoid. Enveloped by constantly moving translucent tendrils. Staring at them from unseen eyes hidden deep within the void of its very being. The light around it was swallowed by the darkness of its presence. It rose up, suspended by the slithering overcoat. The distortion fields suddenly grew in an explosive movement and the darkness vanished. It happened all too fast. As the light returned to the room, McKinney and Duong did not know how to react. For a while longer, they silently stared at the empty and now well-illuminated space next to the bed. The resting place of the shadow being was still very visible. The floor it had lain on. The walls it had touched with its body. It all was distorted and turned into an amalgamation of shapes and forms, most of which McKinney could not even hope to name.

14. Medication

McKinney took a large sip from his cup. He wished the tea in his cup were actually whiskey. However, the food generators in the mess hall were unable to produce any proper alcohol. After all, the crew was required to be at full mental working capacity at all times. At this very moment, he was convinced that his mind would be significantly closer to full working capacity with a good glass of whiskey—or five.

"So what did we actually see?" Duong asked again.

She was sitting across from him. After the incident, they had decided to leave the crew quarters for now and sit in the mess hall. They had gone over this several times, but without success. Of course, they could somewhat describe the event, but what they had actually witnessed was a mystery to them.

"I really have no answers. Except that whatever we saw was not dead," McKinney added as he put his cup on the table.

Duong looked directly at McKinney. "It looked at me. I felt its stare." She paused, "When it stared at me, I felt it in my whole body. I felt how its mind was reaching out to mine."

McKinney shook his head in an attempt to avoid

her ever more intense stare.

"What do you mean?"

"It showed me... a glimpse—an image."

"What kind of image? What can you remember?" McKinney pressed Duong. He knew what the images were, but maybe she had more pieces to the puzzle.

"I cannot remember much. It is all a blur. I saw a strange landscape. It was all very chaotic."

"A dimension where reality never applies..." McKinney muttered to himself.

"Can I join?" It looks like Duong wanted to say something, but Gonzales's voice interrupted her before she could start to form words.

Looking at both of them in turn, he sat down at the table. McKinney noticed that he was clearly exhausted. He had been in the med bay for many hours seeing to Wolf, and it showed.

He looked at them in turn for a while before asking, "Did something else happen that I don't know about?"

McKinney looked at his old friend. The last few weeks had caught up to all of them in a big way. At this point, they all fully understood that they were not alone and that something out there was out to get them. Something unexplainable. Up until now, their efforts had been focused on the struggle for pure survival. They had not spent a single second building up any meaningful defense or protection against the strange shadow beings.

Duong spoke up: "I also had one of those dark things in my room."

Gonzales nodded. "Ian, you did see that there was one of those things in Wolf's room, right?"

McKinney answered, "I saw something, yes."

"So all of us have had one of these... beings in our room?" Gonzales looked around as he spoke.

"I have not," McKinney shook his head. "But I saw them in my dreams."

He wanted to talk about his encounter at the comms array, but something in him decided to omit this fact. He has definitely had one of the most direct contacts with whatever it was. However, his was not with a shadow being, but maybe with one of their contraptions. What he did see was a lot of incoherent images. He wondered if Wolf had spent time with the creatures more directly.

"So they will likely come for you next, McKinney," Duong deduced.

McKinney did not like the sound of that. He looked at Gonzales and then again at Duong, hoping to find an idea or at least a hint in their faces. He did not want to experience such an encounter on this side of the dream. As he thought about it, he became uncertain if his experiences in his dreams had actually been experiences in his dreams. These beings were somewhat able to affect reality even if they had appeared only in his dreams. And then there was his experience with the comms array. He had seen things while he was in there. Things he was still processing. It had been too much. Even with time, he could not put any of it into any meaningful context. Had that been his encounter already? He did not want to risk having another experience like that.

"Let us move our beds into one room. Then one person can stand guard while the other rests, and we take turns." A soldier's idea from a soldier. Duong clearly had the experience they needed most if they had any hope of getting out of this situation alive.

"Linh, that is a great idea." Gonzales jumped up from his seat. He had regained a lot of energy. Maybe it was the fact that he could finally do something productive about the issue. "We should sleep in the med bay, so Wolf won't be alone. It also has enough beds."

It was the most logical choice. McKinney still wished to return to Wolf's room and go through her notes. Might it be possible that he could get some information from Wolf directly?

"Carlos, how is Wolf doing? Do you think we can talk to her?" he asked Gonzales, who was not able to sit anymore and wandered around the table.

"Well, she lost a lot of blood, Ian." Gonzales stopped his pacing for a bit and looked at McKinney. "While I tried to sedate her, she still kept moving her hand as if she were trying to write something. She kept opening the wounds on her fingers by doing that." He made a motion of his fingers scraping on the table. Then he continued his pacing around the table as he spoke. "I wrapped her hands up with thick cloth and tied her arms down to the bed. After a long while, she started to calm down completely. I don't think you will be able to talk to her for quite a while."

So talking to her was not possible. McKinney decided to go to her room as soon as he could and take a look at those papers. He had to find a way to make sense of the barrage of images he had received at the comms array. He felt as if he were carrying some otherworldly large truth with him that he could not access. It was slowly driving him mad.

15. Revelation

It took McKinney quite some time to find a reason to leave the other two without making them suspicious. He needed his own space for this. He did not want to explain himself at the moment. Whenever he was alone, the images came back to him more intensely. A cryptic mess of many lifetimes of impressions. As McKinney walked towards the crew quarters, he tried to focus on singular images. But as always, it seemed impossible. So many images fused, merged, and melded with each other. His head started to hurt, and he stopped his attempt. Something dropped from his nose. He was bleeding again. Too much exhaustion. He paused for a moment before entering the crew quarters section.

The place was still a complete mess. Wolf's room was wide open, and paper, screens, tools, and other debris were lying around everywhere inside and out-side the room. Sorting through this would take quite a while, especially without the guidance of Wolf.

He wanted—no—he needed the information, so he had little choice. He knelt down and started picking up some of the papers. As he looked at some of them, he noticed that they seemed to be empty. The symbols, patterns, notes—it was all gone. He picked up another page—blank. He picked up a screen—wiped. Desperation overcame him. He rushed into the room, picking up page after page, screen after screen. No scribbles, no ink, no text. Everything had vanished. Something within him broke. Angry, he threw the items in his hand against the wall. He took another stack from the floor and threw that one as well. He wanted to scream but stopped himself and instead punched the walls and the floor until his knuckles bled. The numbing effect of the pills kept him from feeling pain. He picked up a large chunk of metal to throw that as well. As he lifted it above his head, his damaged shoulder gave out. He just managed to direct the debris away from himself. As it crashed to the floor, he noticed that the pills could not stop all the pain. Exhausted and in agony, he collapsed to the floor. Tears created a thin stream from his eyes.

As he was lying within the piles of empty paper and dead screens, the images came back to him. At first, he struggled, but he felt weak. He could not hold them back much longer. Then he noticed that the pressure let up. He opened his mind and allowed them to flood in. More and more images, some now clearer than before. He let them all in. Filling his head with the ideas and thoughts of something he did not understand. The images showed something his mind could not unravel alone. He saw landscapes, cities, planets. All of them completely impossible. Dimensions that could not be. Structures that could not exist. Alignments that could not be formed. Buildings that could not be shaped. He saw glimpses of a reality that could not be a reality. An irreality. A dimension where no rules applied. He saw billions of humans throughout time. Sleeping and dreaming. When they dreamed, the veil between reality and irreality became thinner. He saw how shapeless shapes found ways to push through the veil and touch the dreamers' dreams. He finally understood now why it had all started in dreams. Another tear left his eye and ran down his cheek, only to be caught in his red hair. He let himself float and opened up his mind further.

There were so, so unbelievably many glimpses and impressions. So many images and experiences. The pressure grew again. The images became more and more distorted. Overlaps and fusions. Images melted together. He could not concentrate. Blood was again dripping from his nose. The headache became unbearable. He felt as if he were about to lose himself in the information flood. He tried grasping for what was his own memory and what wasn't. He found that a distinction became increasingly more difficult. He opened his eyes. He wanted to scream but stopped himself. He staggered to his feet. He walked around the room. He needed distractions. He was close. In his visions, he had received parts of the message. Maybe he could understand the rest as well. He needed to get back into that mindset, but he didn't know how.

And then he heard screaming, but it wasn't his. It came from somewhere else on the ship.

-◇-

The screams did not really sound human. They sounded wrong, distorted, and agonizingly uncanny. Underneath it all, there was something he recognized. McKinney almost slipped as he ran down the central corridor, following the screams toward the med bay. As he passed through the hatch, he saw Duong and Gonzales were just entering the room as well. McKinney followed Duong through the door and saw that Gonzales was already at Wolf's bed.

As McKinney moved closer, the complete situation was revealed to him. Wolf was sitting upright in bed, screaming almost without catching a breath. Her vocal cords were already overburdened. The sound that exited was distorted as a result. Her mouth was open wide, stretching skin and muscle to their extremes. Eyes stared upwards and the body was tensed up. He was convinced that the only reason she was still in the bed was the straps tying her hands to the bed frame. McKinney wondered if she felt pain. If so, she must have been in immeasurable agony.

Gonzales was already injecting a syringe into her arm. He could barely push the needle through the tense muscles. "I am not sure if any tranquilizer will work here." He screamed over the unbearable sound leaving the throat of Wolf.

McKinney felt helpless. He did not know what to do or how to help. He touched Wolf to see if he could bring her body to lie back down. Upon touching, he realized that her body was as hard as stone. The muscles would rather tear than budge. He looked at Gonzales. He shook his head.

Then suddenly the scream's pitch went up quickly. It then became breathy, and finally the room was drenched in silence. Wolf was still tensed up. Air still left her mouth. But the vocal cords seemed to have been damaged. No further sound was produced aside from the silent, hoarse rattle produced by the sore throat.

It was a relief. McKinney's ears were still ringing and slowly adjusted to the silence that now surrounded him.

"Can you give her more tranq, Carlos?" Duong asked.

"I already gave her the maximum dosage. More could kill her," Gonzales said.

"Well, this will also kill her." She pointed at the stiff, cramped body of Wolf, which still screamed without making a sound.

Gonzales looked at the situation and went to the cabinet to fill another syringe.

In that very moment, Wolf closed her mouth. Still tensed up, she stared at her crew with a painful grin. Her eyes were empty and dead. She then formed words with her mouth. McKinney was closest to her and put his ear right next to her mouth. He could hear slowly spoken pieces of broken sentences as she shaped silent air with her lips and tongue.

"Zor'Xuuth... journey... cut open the wound... now a scar... the prison... a guide."

Zor'Xuuth. That word. It made sense to him, but he did not know why or what it meant. Yet, it sounded so familiar.

She wanted to repeat her sentence when her body suddenly convulsed. Her face became distorted again, but this time it was not the muscles that caused it. Something was moving underneath the skin. McKinney could hear the skull cracking. Finally, she threw back her head as a stream of unidentifiable black matter burst out of her mouth. Her eyes vanished, and the sockets also burst out further streams with a rustling sound. McKinney ducked away.

Gonzales got hit by one of the streams through his hand as he tried to approach Wolf. It went through and fused his arm immediately to his shirt. He screamed and ripped off his sleeve with some tissue from his arm. Bleeding profusely, he punched for the cabinet containing the bandages and grabbed a handful before darting for the door.

The room started to fill with the matter. McKinney began to understand what exactly it was that was leaving Wolf. It was all the symbols from the papers and screens that she had internalized. All the knowledge was now pouring out of her. Whatever it touched immediately started to warp. Reality was bending and breaking around the stream of information. Leaving their captain. It began to attach itself to the hull of the silent prophet and eat away at the material.

Then a loud bang cut through the busy rustling sound of the knowledge leaving the ruptured mind. Wolf's head exploded into a red mist. The black matter instantly stopped reacting. It was now sticking to equipment, the ceiling, and walls like black slime. Slowly, it was dripping downwards into the puddles that were accumulating on the floor. McKinney saw Duong standing at the door with a gun in her hand. The barrel was still smoking. She grabbed his arm with a strength he had not imagined she would possess and pulled him through the pressure door out of the med bay and into the corridor. Then she punched in the button for sealing off the whole section. The pressure door hydraulics hissed aggressively as they pressed the hatch door violently into its frame. They only stopped once it was a perfectly airtight fit.

-◇-

For a long time, nobody spoke a word and nobody moved. They sat together in the corridor in front of the hatch, leaning against the wall. Gonzales was wrapping his arm. The fusing of material had gone deep. Veins and bone were visible on the outside. The hand was completely stiff as the joint would not function anymore. He could still move some of his fingers. The bandage would hold back the bleeding for now.

As he was done, he looked at his work with a dark grin. He stuffed the other bandages into his pocket and stood up.

"We should continue with our plan. Let's get mattresses from the crew quarters and put them in the mess hall." With that, he started down the corridor. Duong also got up and followed him. McKinney looked after them both, but his mind was elsewhere.

Zor'Xuuth... The Riftweaver.

16. Influence

McKinney had lain awake for far too long. Too many things running through his mind had kept him from sleeping. Finally, his exhaustion had caught up with him and pulled him into an uneasy sleep.

His dreams were plagued by the onslaught of images that were ever-present. In his sleep, he had no way of shielding his mind from the barrage of impressions. By now, he understood that these images contained a story that would be his to tell. The story was greater than any human-made tale and more important than his own. He again opened his mind in his sleep to learn more. The images again became clearer. However, this time, they were different. Instead of seeing images from the strange dimension, he saw images from the past.

He saw Nicolas Claude Fabri de Peiresc sleeping in his bed in Aix in November 1610. He watched him through a veil. As his sleep took him into the land of dreams, the veil became thinner and thinner until he saw that glimpses were able to push through and affect his dream. In his dream, Claude was walking along a sunny beach when suddenly the daytime switched to night. A clear starry sky shone brightly down on him. The image turned and zoomed until the Orion Nebula became clearly visible in front of him. Shining bright and colorful.

He saw Galileo Galilei as he dreamed of the trapezium in February of 1617. He was sleeping in his bed in Florence. He saw Christiaan Huygens dreaming of the nebula in 1656. He saw Jean Picard locating the fourth star of the trapezium in 1673.

He understood how humanity was influenced by the shadows of the nebula for millennia. He was here because they wanted him to be here. They had called out, and humanity had finally answered. He was sent. It was his task alone to answer the call.

-◇-

McKinney opened his eyes slowly. It had been a rough night for him, and his dreams were still lingering in his mind. He took a few moments to let his body catch up to him. Slowly, he noticed that his muscles were aching worse than expected. He then noticed that he was not sleeping but sitting. Sitting in a pilot chair. With terror, he tore open his eyes. This was not the mess hall. This was the bridge.

He jumped up from his seat and looked around. He was sitting in the pilot's seat. The entire room was warped. The dashboard and flight controls especially had changed to something else. He could still understand some of what he saw, and what he saw was that a new hop had been initiated. Panic gripped him. His fingers danced across the controls, attempting to figure out how to stop the process. He had no time to figure out the warped and ever-fluctuating controls.

Staring at the screen in disbelief, he saw that the course was locked using his own code. He had done this. He had set the course.

All of a sudden, he felt a calmness wash over him. He had done this for a greater purpose.

McKinney walked toward the mess hall at a brisk speed. He needed to warn the others as soon as he could. The clock was ticking. The jump would start in less than 10 minutes. It was enough time to comfortably get ready, but not enough to take a stroll. He still tried to figure out how exactly he had gotten out without anyone noticing. His memory seemed to start getting gaps. He wondered if that was due to the vast amount of information he had received from the comms array.

As he entered the mess hall, he saw that both Gonzales and Duong were fast asleep in their beds.

He wasted no time and screamed while shaking Gonzales's arm: "Wake up, we have to get ready for the hop!"

Duong was up astonishingly fast. The military background came through. Her alertness was exemplary. Gonzales struggled, especially with his warped arm and the pain emanating from it.

"MyKinney, what happened?" Duong helped Gonzales to his feet while dragging him toward the door.

"I'm not sure. Something brought me to the bridge.

The hop had already started. We have no time. We have to get to the pods."

McKinney's explanation was problematic. Duong looked at McKinney with suspicion in her eyes. McKinney knew she could tell that he did not tell the complete truth. But he pushed on. He wanted to avoid any conflict.

When they entered the pod room, McKinney did not feel great about the situation. Too much had gone horribly wrong here, and this time it was likely even more dangerous. But his doubts were somehow swallowed by a feeling of calmness in his mind. Something within him told him that everything was as it should be. And what choice did they have? Outside of the pods awaited certain death during the hop.

He looked around and saw Duong helping Gonzales into his pod. Gonzales did not do well. His old friend was in agony.

He was not surprised to see that this room was also in flux. Constantly warping just a little bit. Not enough to call this room defunct, but certainly enough to make guessing exact distances and shapes nearly impossible.

He climbed into his pod and closed the canopy. Duong passed him by on the way from Gonzales's pod to hers and looked at him. She knew something was not right. That much was obvious.

He was eagerly awaiting the sedative to pull him out of this reality and into a dream.

17. Incursion

McKinney watched the countdown and began to feel nervous. Usually by now the sedative would already have been administered. Yet, it did not happen. He kept watching the clock, awaiting sleep.

30 SECONDS

He was still wide awake. He turned his head sideways as far as the cushions allowed him. He could barely see Duong, who was attempting the same. He could see the desperation in her eyes. Without a sedative, this residual pain from the transition could be felt. McKinney started to shake internally.

20 SECONDS

McKinney braced for the pain he would inevitably feel. The sedative was still not administered, and by now it would not matter anymore.

18 SECONDS

Then the whole room warped, shifted, and

distorted. Reality seemed to break as shapes suddenly turned into animated shadows. Tendrils lashed out of distorted air and reached into the darkness. With sudden, unearthly strength, the tendrils tore shapes from the shadows and lifted them up in the air.

The bright red light of the monitor displaying the clock lit up the shadow beings from behind. It cut their shapes out of the otherwise dark surroundings. McKinney could see their bodies for the first time. The tendrils were much less enveloping the creatures as they were cocooning them in a living, morphing net of thin strings. They looked vaguely humanoid, although they did not seem to have legs. It looked more as if the spindly, warping torso ended in thicker pockets of the cocoon that vaguely took the shape of incomplete legs. They had skinny arms of a length McKinney could not estimate as they seemed to shift constantly. There was an oval shape where humans would have a head. McKinney thought he saw gleaming eyes in the void of the oval head. It made the head shape look like a window to distant stars in a night sky.

15 SECONDS

The shadow beings moved with unreal speed. Tendrils spread from their fingers and started warping around Gonzales's pod. McKinney could hear muffled screams.

10 SECONDS

Out of the corner of his eye, McKinney could see how Gonzales's pod started to change dramatically. Openings were created. Atoms were rearranged to change the overall structure of the pod.

5 SECONDS

The Shadow beings had completed their task, and the tendrils vanished. What was left was a contraption that McKinney could not understand at first glance.

2 SECONDS

The beings looked at McKinney and Duong and moved over to Duong's pod.

1 SECOND

Tendrils spread out. The shadow beings started to build a web around Duong's pod.

With a powerful eruption that shocked the entire ship like an earthquake, the FTL engines came alive. McKinney felt his body being torn apart by incredible forces. The room before him was ripped out of time and space and warped into a spiral shape as the atoms were pushed into a different continuum. The pain was far worse than McKinney had ever imagined. The shadow beings around Duong's pod were wiped from his vision. McKinney did not know if they had left or died. Her pod seemed to be functional. Yet, he saw how her face started to reflect the same agony he was feeling.

He moved his head to his right and forced his eyes to open. He could barely make out how Gonzales's pod started to disintegrate. The forces broke down the pod to its most basic molecular structures and with it, Gonzales. There was no screaming, just silent acceptance as Gonzales got pulled apart atom by atom. He looked over to McKinney with a face filled with a mixture of agony, exhaustion, and relief. Tears ran down McKinney's face as the pain pulled his consciousness into the darkness, and McKinney passed out.

18. Desperation

Through the pain-induced coma, McKinney could not remember if he had dreamed during the hop. He also did not have any recollection of how long he had passed out. Slowly, McKinney opened his eyes. His vision was blurry. Every muscle in his body cramped. After a few moments, he managed to focus his eyes and look around. The room had changed dramatically. It was now fully transformed into a surreal environment. Underneath the constantly fluctuating surfaces, he could still see the reminders of what the room used to look like. The red light of the screen was seeping through a layer of cryptic symbols. These made up a distortion field that was moving in unknowable directions, fluctuating in scale and shape. Wolf's pod was fully fused with the ship into a mound of different materials that seemed both too large and too small at the same time. The complete floor seemed structurally sound but also uneasy to walk on.

Slowly, he gathered himself. The canopy of his pod was already open. After peeling himself out of the cushioning of his pod, he fell to the ground. His legs had given out, and he decided to rest before attempting the next step.

Duong placed a hand on him. The sudden pressure made him jump inside a little. As he turned around, he could see that she was already wide awake. Her face did not show any signs of strain or pain. She was just built differently.

"Are you ok?" She asked.

"Yes... Give me a minute. This was rough." He answered quickly.

Duong tapped his shoulder and stood up. Looking into the direction of the missing pod that Gonzales had been in.

"Did you see what happened?" Now her voice showed a sliver of sadness. While she spoke, she stepped over McKinney toward where the pod had been.

McKinney was too exhausted to choose his words carefully. "The beings, they did something to his pod. During the job, it malfunctioned. Gonzales... he... " McKinney's feelings finally caught up to him, and he was not able to finish the sentence.

Duong knelt at the spot where Gonzales's pod had been. She placed one hand on the connection joint that had remained as the last piece of evidence that a pod had ever been present here. McKinney heard her sob. The first time her soldier mask had fully cracked. He had no recollection of them having gotten that close. It came as a complete surprise to him. He could hardly remember Gonzales and Duong having gotten closer—or was he missing something? He tried searching his memory. More pieces had gone missing.

His time at the academy was almost completely wiped. He only remembered that he had been there. McKinney slowly got up from the floor and walked over to Duong. He did not know what was appropriate here, so he settled for placing a hand on her shoulder just as she had done before. After a few moments, she got up and hugged him.

Then she whispered in his ear: "I think I can hear him. He's still here!"

A shiver went down McKinney's spine. That was completely impossible... But after everything he had seen, maybe it was possible.

"How can you hear him?" he asked softly.

"He is inside the ship, calling for me. Can't you hear him too?"

McKinney couldn't.

"I... I don't know," he tried.

"Shhh!" she said softly as she loosened her hug. She took his arm and pulled him closer to where the pod had been. "You must listen closely!"

Her grip became unnaturally strong. McKinney winced and decided that the fastest way to get out of this situation would be to play along. He stared into the empty space in front of him.

"Yes, I can hear him," McKinney lied.

"No, you must listen." There was something off in her voice. She did not let up. She saw through his lie. Her grip became stronger. McKinney struggled.

"Please let me go. It really hurts." He tried shaking her off. But her grip only got tighter. He tried shaking away from her, but her hands had a tight grip on him. He felt like he was being held by a vice.

"Listen!" Her voice sounded coarse and deep. It did not sound like her voice.

"There is nothing here! Let go of me," he screamed.

"Ian, are you there? I cannot see. It is so dark!" Gonzales's voice sounded hollow and far away.

McKinney froze in shock. He could feel his heart beating in his head. He noticed how Duong's muscle strength softened to a human level. Then she let go of him.

Hundreds of thoughts raced through his mind. Gonzales, his old friend. He had forgotten since when he had known him. How had they become friends? He had forgotten Gonzales's face. What did he look like? McKinney broke out in a cold sweat. Panic gripped him.

He raced out of the room into the central corridor. He was mostly stumbling as his feet had issues understanding the distance to the fluctuating floor. Suddenly, a bright beam cut through the darkness surrounding the ship. It blazed a trail of glistening light through the windows of the bridge all the way down the central corridor. He was grabbed from behind and pulled back into the pod room just as the beam of unbelievably bright light blazed past him. Duong pulled him to the side and forced his face toward the wall. His eye still hurt from the brightness. He needed time to recover, but he wanted to be out of this room as fast as possible.

"McKinney, are you ok?" She asked.

He stared at her. Desperately trying to focus his eyes again. His efforts seemed to be in vain. The beam had damaged his sight.

-◇-

Several more light beams passed by. Each one drenching the room in glistening light. McKinney and Duong had drawn back into a corner where the light could barely reach. McKinney was trying to refocus his eyes, but he had no doubt that damage had been done.

"What happened to you?" he asked her.

"What do you mean?" Her voice was soft and silent. She spoke slowly.

"You almost broke my arm!" An accusation. He felt angry.

"What are you talking about?" she asked, looking at him with a puzzled expression.

Did it actually happen? He could barely remember her holding him so tightly. Aside from the general soreness, his body also had no recollection of what had happened. Did he only imagine her strength? Things here did not fully function as he would assume. Was this the effect of the influence of the irreality? Was the man, Gonzales, also part of the irreality? Did he actually hear him? Did he ever exist? Somehow, these thoughts started forming in his mind as he waited.

He understood that he needed to get out of this

room. He had to see the nebula, even if it would just be blurry. The colors would be enough to make him feel her warm embrace. The thought excited him. He noticed that he suddenly smiled. Something told him that it was safe to go now. He felt stronger again. His muscles still ached, but he was able to ignore them for the most part.

"Duong, the beams seem to have stopped. We should go to the bridge and see what is going on." He tapped Duong on the shoulder.

She reacted instantly, but something was different. Her movements had slowed down. Tears had coated her eyes. The soldier in her had cracked underneath the pressure. Yet, McKinney barely noticed it. His mind was somewhere else. Images came flooding back into his mind. He needed to understand all of it. The solution was in the nebula. He had to see it. How much he would be able to see did not matter to him. Without minding Duong any further, he stepped out of the room and walked toward the bridge. Duong followed him at a slight distance.

As he stepped into the room, he already knew what his eyes could barely make out. They were deep inside the nebula. Dead center between the four stars that made up the trapezium. He stepped closer to the window. He needed to see more. Curse these eyes that failed him. It was all here. He knew it as more and more images flooded his mind and melded with the blurry information his eyes provided.

He suddenly saw from the corner of his eye another

bright beam coming directly at him. Without warning, he dropped to the floor and pressed his face into the distorted flight control console. He could still see the bright light as it pierced through the window. He heard a violent scream. As the beam passed on, he turned around. Behind him on the floor, he saw Duong. Her eyes burned out of their sockets, her skin slightly scorched—but she was still alive. He crept towards her. She was in a delirium. Her lips were moving.

As he got closer he could hear her whisper: "Carlos... where is Carlos... he is here, he is waiting for m... me... He is in the prison of the Tar'En..."

Tar'En - McKinney remembered that name. He didn't know if it was his memory or a memory given to him. It did not matter. He knew the shadow beings by name. Their name was Tar'En. Another piece of his puzzle. McKinney felt happy. He started to understand it all.

Again, he allowed more images to flood his mind. With new information, maybe he could see more in the images. New memories formed, and old ones were removed. Unnecessary baggage that could all be discarded.

McKinney was torn from his thoughts as Duong jumped up.

"Carlos, he is at the airlock. I have to get to him!" she screamed at McKinney and stumbled for the door. Her memory of the layout guided her but did not prevent her from hitting walls, chairs, and falling over her feet. She adjusted. Feeling her way through the darkness that was now her home.

Still being half dazed, he did not fully understand the commotion. But he understood that the airlock would lead out. It would lead him closer to the nebula. Slowly, he got up and followed her. She had already reached the far end of the corridor as McKinney made it through the door of the bridge. Bolting toward her, he could see her struggling to open the airlock. He noticed something was wrong. She was not wearing her spacesuit. McKinney increased his walking speed.

"Stop! What are you doing!" He screamed as Duong entered the airlock and closed the door behind her.

He watched through the small window in the door as Duong opened the opposing hatch. She turned back and looked in his direction. He felt an eternal sorrow emanating from her. A desperate smile crossed her lips. McKinney screamed as he watched Duong slowly suffocating as the air cycled. Her veins grew and tore open as the air expanded in the vacuum. Her body froze as it was slowly drifting out of the airlock into space. Against the bright colors of the nebula, he saw how her silhouette was slowly vanishing. His eyes failed him in displaying the details, and he was glad for it. He sank against the door.

Now it was just him.

He was alone.

Nobody could now take the nebula away from him. Nobody could take away the warm embrace of his mother.

He ended the air cycle and went to the closet next to the door to grab his suit.

McKinney put on his suit. His ceremonial garment.

He had waited for this moment for a long time.

He now understood: it was a reunion with old friends.

He stepped into the airlock and closed the door behind him. The air cycled, and slowly the outer door opened. McKinney stepped out into the nebula. In the distance, he could see each of the bright, shining stars of the Trapezium at an equal distance.

He was here.

Mother, I am ready!

With his blurry vision, he could see the Tar'En coming for him.

19. dnE

McKinney felt the webbing enclose his body as the Tar'En worked around him. The world around him grew dark. Then he felt the webbing of the tendrils tighten around him. Embracing him softly and lifting him up softly. His blurry vision gave little hint as to where he was being taken. He felt the cold breeze rush over his skin. A distortion portal transported him, and the world around him went black.

When he opened his eyes, he found himself back in the landscape. The promise that had been made to start this expedition. The fuel that had brought the silent prophet all this way. Now it was a distorted irreality. Gone were the luscious greens and evaporated was the crystal clear water. The blue sky was enshrouded in a cloud made of colors McKinney could not begin to name. In its center, a tear had gone through the sky that had grown back together. In front of the tear, a massive cloud was constantly moving and shifting.

McKinney knew he would not need the suit here. He removed his helmet to get a better view of his surroundings. It did not help much. He could not understand. He tried to see, to focus. The images in his head started spinning out of control. He knew what he needed to see was not something meant for human eyes to witness. It was not something a human mind could decipher. He closed his eyes, tried to feel the irreality. He could not. The darkness in front of his eyes was still reporting false information. In desperation, he contorted his body to find a shadow darker than his closed eyes could deliver. He needed to transcend the limitations of his mortal shell. Nothing seemed to work. He cried out in anger and frustration. The answers were here. He could feel their presence, but they stayed out of reach.

In a fit of rage, he took his fingers to his eyes and pulled them out of their sockets. Blood was spurting from the depths of his skull. The pain numbed his mind. The veil that had covered his sight was finally gone and he saw...

... Everything!

He saw the desperate god of irreality Zor'Xuuth. A being of boundless age and unfathomable knowledge. Knowledge unreal and unsorted. Its frantic cry shook a universe. Attracted to the blissful order granted by reality, it tore a rift into time and space. Like remoras, the Tar'En had to follow their god through the rift. Without it, irreality would collapse. Their lives now tethered to Zor'Xuuth, as only in its presence were beings of irreality able to exist in reality. An inescapable cage built from a will to survive. To exist. To persist.

As Zor'Xuuth, the rift weaver, rested from its task. As it dreamed its mind would reach out in bright beams of endless light that cut through the darkness like swords. The rift slowly healed and became a scar. The leaked irreality became a nebula in space. To the Tar'En, it was a prison. Over millions of years, the Tar'En would search for an escape from their prison. They knew they needed a being that could exist in reality and irreality alike. And they found humanity. Too far away for direct contact. But in their dreams, the veil between irreality and reality became thin, and the Tar'En started to influence humanity.

McKinney looked up. Where the massive cloud had previously been now loomed a massive being that was constantly shifting in and out of existence. Its body seemed to be fighting for its presence in reality. It was impossible to grasp its shape and scale. He only saw it because his mind could feel the incomprehensible power emanating from Zor'Xuuth. Here it had been dormant and resting for almost two billion human years. From it, uncountable tendrils sprouted in all directions. Tethers to the Tar'En. Needed by them to survive.

He was here as he had proven himself worthy. His crewmates had been insufficient for the task at hand.

I understand now.

The tethers fell from Zor'Xuuth. The Tar'En approached him from all sides.

Yes! I will be your guide! I will care for you!

His mind became their host. His body no longer existed purely in reality.

-◇-

He was back on the ship. He saw so much more without his eyes limiting him. He finally understood the controls and the concept. He went to the bridge and set a course. He did not need to calculate where to go next. He saw it. He did not need the hop pods. His body could warp with reality.

He sat down in the captain's chair. In his head were the voices and knowledge of billions of years and millions of minds.

END

Epilogue

It was in the middle of the night. Commander Gruber had built an understanding of being called to base at such an ungodly hour over the years, but it was never pleasant. His wife was still sleeping as he struggled into his pants and almost fell down the stairs. A coffee was definitely in order once he got to base. He hurried to his car and almost fell over Pippin, their Newfoundland dog that blended in perfectly with the lawn in the darkness. As he got into his car, he was thinking of ways to better illuminate that dog.

He raced down the short road from his home to mission control. The streetlights were off at this hour, and the air was brutally cold. It was one of those nights he wished he had not signed up for.

As he reached the gate, the guard stopped him and checked his ID. They knew each other, but the process was the same no matter the rush.

Gruber drove into the parking lot at the far end of the gigantic mission control building. Now it was just a short jog into the warm hands of the coffee machine.

Has he finally opened the door to mission control with a cup of delicious coffee in his hands. He found the place in disarray. Immediately, Avery Clark approached him. He had been responsible for the night shift at mission control for many years. Gruber knew him as a very trustworthy and diligent worker. Today, he was in shambles.

"Commander, you have to see this... This is impossible!" he almost screamed as he spoke. Gruber shielded his coffee with his hand against potential spit. The wild gestures made him look at the massive screen covering the far side of the room.

There, in red letters, he read:

FTL SHIP SILENT PROPHET REQUESTING EMERGENCY LANDING.

He dropped his coffee. This was impossible! The Silent Prophet had been lost nearly 10 years earlier. He looked at Clark, who looked back at him.

Then his voice roared like thunder through the hall: "Initiate landing protocol!"